Hoffmann

PATRICIA C. MCKISSACK

FREDRICK L. MCKISSACK

JOHN MCKISSACK

CYBORG

THE SECOND BOOK OF THE CLONE CODES

SCHOLASTIC PRESS
NEW YORK

All rights reserved. Published by Scholastic Press, an imprint of Scholastic Inc., *Publishers since 1920.* SCHOLASTIC, SCHOLASTIC PRESS, and associated logos are trademarks and/or registered trademarks of Scholastic Inc.

Library of Congress Cataloging-in Publication Data

McKissack, Patricia, 1944–

Cyborg : a Clone Codes novel / Patricia C. McKissack, Fredrick L. McKissack, John McKissack. — 1st ed. p. cm.

Summary: Seventeen-year-old Houston, a cyborg since the age of seven, and a fugitive living on the Moon, joins with other cyborgs all over the world in non-violent protest marches to challenge the Cyborg Act of 2130 and hopefully secure increased civil liberties.

ISBN 978-0-439-92985-1

[1. Science fiction.   2. Cyborgs — Fiction.
3. Artificial intelligence — Fiction.   4. Civil rights movements — Fiction.]   I. McKissack, Fredrick.   II. McKissack, John.   III. Title.

PZ7.M478693Cy 2011
[Fic] — dc22
2010016075

10 9 8 7 6 5 4 3 2 1 11 12 13 14 15

Printed in the United States of America   23

First edition, February 2011
Book design by Phil Falco

JPM

To Mom Bess, my grandmother (the Past)

To Michelle, my amore (the Present)

To my great-great-grandchildren (the Future)

PCM & FLM, Sr.

To Mother (the Past)

To Robert and Fred, Jr. (the Present)

To our great-great-grandchildren (the Future)

A GUIDE TO THE CYBORG UNIVERSE
Published by the Bureau of Cyborg Affairs
Chamber of Commerce, Visitor Division

Here is the standard as defined by The World Federation of Nations. We are an enforcement group. Our primary purpose is to educate, monitor, and uphold the rules and standards of our homelands so that we can maintain a system of clearly defined roles among our residents. We have created this guide as a means for our visitors to know exactly where they stand, and as an easy reference for complying with the laws we have set forth.

What Is a Cyborg?

By order of The World Federation of Nations (The WFN), as of January 1, 2084, all persons who have been enhanced with three or more biofe, or synthetic body or organ replacements, shall be classified as three-fifths of a human being, or a cyborg. The conversion to a cyborg makes one uncivilized.

Cyborgs do not feel things to the same extent as humans. Some cyborgs have the ability to express or internalize their emotions, but this is dependent on what percentage of their bodies is synthetic.

The Cyborg Act of 2130

For the security and general welfare of the cyborg race, these protections have been established on this 7th day of October, 2130.

John P. Haversham
Director of the Bureau of Cyborg Affairs

THE CYBORG ACT

- All cyborgs must be registered with the Bureau of Cyborg Affairs (BCA).

- Those that are cyborgs must live within designated areas set aside on the Moon Colony. If a cyborg desires to live or work elsewhere, it must acquire BCA permission.

- It is mandated that cyborgs may not serve as officers in the World Federation of Nations' defense forces, serve in any national law enforcement agencies, or hold public office.

- Cyborg children must attend one of four cyborg academies based on test scores and abilities.

- All cyborgs over the age of 16 must be employed.

- Cyborgs need permission from the BCA to marry or have children.

- The BCA will provide cyborgs with medical insurance and health-care needs.

- Cyborgs cannot inherit real property.

- Cyborgs can only participate in amateur or professional sports within the Cyborg Leagues.

The highest order of human beings, Firsts, is a superior race. Firsts are all human. Firsts have the most advanced level of brain function — emotional capability and reasoning power. Firsts are smarter, cleaner, quicker, and more advanced than all other beings.

THE WHOLERS

The Wholers are a human supremacy group. The Wholer philosophy is that any human with even one artificial body part is not pure and therefore unacceptable. Wholer cells are first generation. Wholers consider themselves to be supreme beings — whole, pure, nothing synthetic. All Wholers are Firsts, but all Firsts are not Wholers. Under the recently passed Wholer Act, anyone with as little as one synthetic body part — but still considered a First — is now classified as a cyborg.

CLONES

Clones constitute the lowest order of humanoid. Clones have second-generation cells. They are inferior and are called Seconds. They are replicas of humans only in their physical makeup. Clones are not capable of feeling emotions. They cannot reason or think abstractly. Clones are owned by Firsts for the purpose of labor. Clones are living organisms patented by Topas Corporation International. Clones are governed by the laws of the Clone Codes, issued by the Clone Humane Society, the government agency for the protection and processing of clones. Under the auspices of the

THE CLONE CODES

▮ All clones are to be identified by number or alphanumerical designation. The use of names is restricted.

▮ Clones have no rights under a court of law and are recognized solely as property.

▮ Groups of clones in excess of three are not permitted without direct human supervision.

▮ Attempting to educate a clone beyond its work model specifications is forbidden and punishable in accordance with article 3C74.

▮ The manufacture of a clone in the likeness of a child is a capital offense.

▌ Imprinting the ability to mimic human emotions
into a clone's behavioral patterns is forbidden.

▌ A clone that disobeys a direct order must
immediately be taken to a processing center
for decommissioning.

▌ Instructing a clone to lie is restricted.

▌ Since clones are not citizens, they may not
participate in elections.

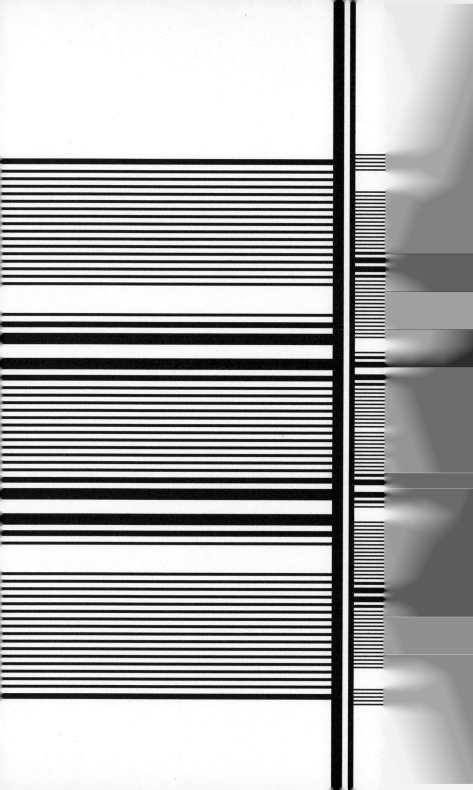

PART ONE

THE YEAR — 2161

BIOFE BOY

I'm seven years old.

We're at Lake Omashski, one of the most remote regions left in Canada.

There's a thunderstorm rolling in, but Mom wants to get one more shot of the wildlife in the area. From where we sit in the boat, her camera lens is aimed toward a red wolf studying us from the lakeshore, resting under these angry skies. "Look, Huey," she says to me, "that's a red wolf. They're supposed to be extinct, but we've actually spotted one." Mom's excited. She's hardly bothered by the storm.

The winds whip. They're as angry as the skies, and fighting, too, against the thunder's growl. I have to squint to see the wolf. From what I can see, it's a beautiful animal. So focused and graceful. Its eyes never leave us. And it almost looks like the wolf's gaze is only on me. He's staring. He's got his eyes locked on where I am. "Hey," I say softly, as if he and I are speaking to each other.

Lightning flashes all around us. My cousin Jake stands up sharply in our boat. He's scared of the thunder. My other *cousin, Rob, tries to stop Jake from jostling the boat. "Sit down, Jake — please," Rob is pleading.*

Jake and Rob tilt the boat, and both tumble out. Jake falls, headfirst. Rob is knocked by the unsteady boat and lands in the water with a hard smack.

"Jake! Rob!" I reach for them, but they're being swept away by the swift-moving current. I can't snatch either of them back. They're each washed away quickly. Swallowed into the black lake. Gone so fast. "Rob! Jake!" I'm screaming with all I've got.

Mom can't row the boat in the storm. The winds are too strong.

Dad and my older brother, Toby, are on the other shore, running to keep up with our boat, which is heading for the rapids.

Mom and I get caught in the rapids, moving, turning. . . . Mom's oar flies from her hand. Flips right at my head with a thud. I'm knocked sideways, then down. Then over the falls!

Next thing I know, there are strangers talking above me, telling me to be still. "You're going to be okay," I hear somebody say. The pain in my chest tells me otherwise. "You're lucky to be alive." Oh, yeah? The pain I feel in my arm and leg is unbearable. I hear people telling me Mom tried to grab my leg, but the water was too fierce. Telling me Toby started to swim out, tried to save me. But Dad wouldn't let him go too far.

We're back at our campsite now. It's hard for me to breathe as I hear all this. Mom is crying. Toby's just quiet. Not talking. Looking only at the ground.

Dad returns with two old transplant doctors who've come

from a neighboring town. They've agreed to treat me. I remember being moved to their clinic, but I'm still delirious from the accident. All of me feels heavy. I'm afraid I might die. I see my parents struggling with the idea of doing what's available in this place, which would doom me to a life of segregation, prejudice, limited choices, rejection. "What's the boy's name?" one of the doctors asks Mom and Dad.

I start to say my name, but I'm too weak to even talk. Toby answers for me. "His name is Huey."

The doctor administers an injection, and I'm out again.

I wake up blinking hard, trying to make sense of things. Nothing's in focus at first, then everything's sharp in front of me.

I have a biofe eye, a biofe arm and leg, and a new artificial heart.

I'm a cyborg!

Doctors have installed a computer chip in my arm that reports my whereabouts and my life status to the Bureau of Cyborg Affairs.

I'm still a little kid, so it doesn't bother me at first. But as I get older — ten, twelve, fourteen — I hate the idea of being monitored like a criminal. Mom hates it, too. She and Dad fight more. Mom starts to pull away from me. Not talking. Treating me like some kind of dirty burden in her life. She convinces Dad to send me away to a boarding school for cyborg children. When I come home one winter break, Mom's gone. So is Toby.

Months later, Dad dies in a farcar accident, and I'm alone.

Dad had stood by Li Rizin when he became a battlefield cyborg. So Uncle Li becomes my guardian. My only family. My life is not my own now, and I'm scared.

PART TWO
THE YEAR — 2170

ABOMINATIONS

Secrets.

Lies.

Stealing time.

History.

Half-truths.

Whole confessions?

So many questions . . .

This is the reality I live in. This is my map. Call it what you want. I call it the road to me. The life of Houston Ye — a cyborg kid who'll never be a First, a full human. I can't change that. Ever.

Cyborgs are hated in our society — shunned. We're feared because of our superior strength and called all kinds of names like metal heads and staple sticks.

And abominations.

Well, say whatever. I know who I am. I'm more than three-fifths of a human. I can see and feel and hear things humans can't. My biofe eye takes me to inner dimensions of feeling and insight. Yeah, that's right. I'm a cyborg. Talk about me. Stomp on my identity. I'll show you what I'm made of, and it ain't junk. Ask Leanna. She'll tell you. I'm no *abomination*, and neither is she.

SHACKLETON

What have I gotten myself into? I've hijacked a Federation super-spaceship named RUBy! And with an illegal clone and a boy genius, fled to the Moon, where my guardian, Li Rizin, is the manager of mining. The World Federation of Nations wants to arrest us, so it's a matter of time before the security troops will be here. Until then, the Moon is home.

The Moon. The mining camp is mostly underground, sprawling over several miles and connected by tunnels and domes. Above us is the sister city to Atlantis, the biosphere we just escaped from.

Here the biosphere, called Shackleton City, is constructed like a big flowerpot with a teacup-shaped dome sitting on top of it. The whole city is placed in the center of the Moon's Shackleton Crater, securely inside, where it's protected from asteroids and other space debris.

Next to Shackleton are other craters. The largest is the Pole-Aitken Basin, a big hole in the ground the size of Australia. In some places it's 1,500 miles wide and deeper than the oceans of Earth. That's where miles and miles of underground mines and tunnels are located. Rizin says Moon mining is the backbone of the world economy, and even though Rizin is a cyborg — and no friend of the Federation — he gets the job done, so they tolerate him.

Li Rizin, the legendary base mining manager and the first cyborg to hold such a responsible position, supervises 1,900 cyborg miners and laborers. A First by the name of Lawson Keefer, but better known as Big House, was appointed to serve as governor by the WFN Moon Operations Committee back when it started. But Big House and Rizin have an under-standing. Rizin runs the place. And nobody questions him; nobody challenges him. Especially me.

RIZIN AND GRAHAM

On the way to RUBy's lounge deck, where we escapees gather, I'm still thinking about where I am and how I got here. This is not my first visit to the Moon. I spent some of the best times here during vacations from school. Playing sports with my friends Tools and Stick was always special. They taught me everything I know about swifting, my favorite sport. No hope of me ever playing for a pro team, but I've gotten over that hurt. I'm happy to know that I'm as good as a pro. Anyway, I've got a ton of memories. Sometimes when I got lonely at school, I turned on my memory stick and soaked up all the fun and happiness I experienced here on the Moon.

The Moon is a strange place. It takes a lot of getting used to.

Okay. Like, I keep forgetting that on Earth we measure time by the Sun — light and darkness. We normally eat at noon-time, when the Sun is at its highest peak in the sky. When the Sun sets, we call it nighttime and we are trained to sleep. Here at Shackleton, the Sun is always in a dark sky.

Even the term "sky" takes on new meaning around here. When you look through the dome over the structure, it's like being wrapped in a beautiful black blanket. Yet the Sun, with its blinding light, shares the inky space. It's weird and awesome at the same time.

When we arrived on the Moon, Rizin reminded us to use solar visors to look at the Sun, so we wouldn't be blinded. "Closing your eyes won't help, either," he said. "And, Houston, your biofe eye won't protect you," he added sternly.

Rizin is very strict about following rules — his rules. Yet he doesn't care about Federation laws and breaks them whenever he gets a chance. Rizin hates Taylor Graham. Period. Seems it all started when Rizin, Taylor Graham, Joe Spiller, who is a clone bounty hunter and enforcer, and my dad were in the Federation Special Forces together. The details are sketchy, but something went wrong among them. This I know, however: Anything that Graham and Spiller approve, Rizin is sure to be against.

Like — up here, cyborgs, clones, and Firsts live, eat, work, and play together. Rizin insists on this. On Earth, Graham would have a flying fit if cyborgs dared to mingle with Firsts. But here on the Moon nobody cares who you hang out with. It's cool to be friends with whoever you want.

It doesn't matter that Leanna's a clone, Carlos is a runaway First, and RUBy is an Artificial Intelligence. We accept who we are. I can kid around with Leanna openly and nobody cares. I can even joke out loud and not worry about it.

We've been staying on board RUBy, the super-spaceship we escaped in, because there's more to do here. Fringing with my fellow escapees has kept it from being too boring. I slap my hands together the way I do when I'm looking for something to get into. Okay. Leanna looks too comfortable; I think I'll start some jazz with her.

"What's up, Ten-Ten?"

"Don't call me that disgusting name," Leanna says, shooting me an eye dart followed by a smirk. I love cracking on Leanna Deberry. She's such an easy target.

See, Leanna's a clone who wasn't manufactured by the Topas Corporation like all other clones. She grew up thinking she was a First. A First is anyone who has first-generation cells. Clones have second-generation cells and are called Seconds. They're called other names, too, like stupid, throwaways, dumb-dumbs, and Crayola creatures. None of that applies to Leanna. She isn't one of those hideous clone colors — she has hair and a very good mind. In fact, when I met her on board a Gypsy City, I thought she was a First. Funny thing, she thought I was a First, too.

Actually, Leanna is part of an experiment to prove that infant cloning is possible, and if given equal opportunities, clones could be like any other child, able to grow, learn, and function the same as any other human.

The Federation's Clone Humane Society calls Leanna an illegal. Man, talk about crap! But unfortunately, it's true.

Leanna's a fugitive. Her mother, Dr. Annette Deberry, and Dr. Anatol Ayala, Leanna's pediatrician, are members of The Liberty Bell Movement, which launched the infant-clone experiment. The Liberty Bell was called subversive, and Leanna's mother and doctor were arrested as traitors to the Federation.

Leanna makes a perfect case for the legal argument that clones can be sentient beings if not altered by the Topas Corporation during their production. The Federation and Topas will do anything to stop that trial from reaching the World Supreme Court. But Leanna, in order to keep it happening, has to hide before her trial. So she's disguised herself as a typical clone, complete with purple skin and no hair. She even has a numbered name, too — Ten-Ten. She hates it!

As far as Graham and his people are concerned, Leanna's a criminal, and so am I for helping her escape Earth's Clone Codes. Leanna's got a million-dollar bounty on her head. Yeah, that's right. Call her a Second, but at least she's worth a bundle of money.

"What's this? Reading . . . again? Don't you know it's against the law for clones to have pocket readers?" I snap at Leanna, trying not to laugh.

"Benjamin Franklin once told me, 'It is better to read and know that you don't know than to not read and think you know everything,'" she says, never looking away from her reader. "And my name is Leanna, not a number."

"Who's that Benjamin Franklin guy anyway?" I come back defensively. "Is he one of your historical biographs that you keep locked away in your commglasses?"

"Oh, Houston," she says with that blow-off wave of her hand.

I drop my head in mock defeat. "I should know who he is, but I just don't. My school was light on history — it was more like a holding station until we were old enough to work the mines or take some other dangerous job no First wanted," I explain.

Just then RUBy flashes on with a yellow screen. "Good day, everybody," she says, real perky.

Carlos comes bounding into the ship's lounge deck. He's full of energy. No doubt he's ready for anything that leads to an adventure.

CARLOS AND RUBY

Carlos Pace and RUBy. What a pair. Carlos is not your typical ten-year-old. He's a genius, capable of programming a starship as sophisticated as RUBy. Rythonium, Uranius 2He, and Byolythy are the metals that make up RUBy's structure and form the acronym that is her name: RUBy. Most of her metals are Moon mined. In fact, Byolythy was found here.

Carlos programmed the ship with a girl's voice. RUBy even giggles. But don't get confused — RUBy's no kid.

Carlos thinks stealing RUBy from the World Federation of Nations Interplanetary Fleet Development Agency was frisk to the third power. But when I look back over what's hap-pened the past month, from our time together on Earth until now, on the Moon, I get the feeling that RUBy wanted to escape as much as we did; but much more than that, I feel nobody could've stopped her once she'd made up her mind.

But how can an Artificial Intelligence "make up its mind" about anything? AI's are programmed computers. RUBy doesn't come across as a lifeless thing, though. RUBy seems more capable, more powerful than any of us might imagine, except for Carlos and his father, Dr. Marcus Pace. I wonder what they know. I can't believe she is simply a program designed by a ten-year-old boy wonder. There are a lot of unanswered questions I have about Carlos and RUBy.

"I've got a message from Rizin," Carlos shouts. His eyes are bright and full of curiosity. Although Carlos is a genius and capable of marvels, at other times he's like any average kid. That makes him likable. Almost like a little brother. He reminds me of me with my big brother, who I haven't seen in years. "RUBy has downloaded an old ship's log and a biography that explain why this Moon base is named Shackleton City."

"The crater is named Shackleton Crater," I say, real matter-of-fact.

"True, but there's a story about how that name was selected for both the crater, and later, the biosphere. Rizin wants us to read it."

"In school I read about Sir Ernest Shackleton and his expedition on the continent of Antarctica," says Leanna. "Good story."

"I read it in virtual," Carlos adds. "The bravery of the crew and the strength and endurance of their captain are so — "

"Don't tell me," I say, pretending to be interested. Truth is, how much I care about Shackleton getting its name can be measured in micrometers. But this is an assignment from Rizin and I dare not disobey. "All right, let's get going with my daily history lesson," I say, managing a laugh.

"Good! It shouldn't take more than a couple of hours." Leanna pulls her commmglasses off and prepares to leave.

"Where are you going?" I ask.

"I have an errand that must be done by dinnertime. So I'm out of here." She hangs a smile on the last word, making it sound so innocent. She's leaving me here with the kid, alone, to listen to a boring history lesson.

"Wish I could stay," she says, sounding way too sincere. "But I have to go." And she's out of here.

I sigh. "Okay. Seems like it's you and me, kid."

"You and RUBy," corrects Carlos. And like that, he leaves, too.

I'm all alone with RUBy. I don't have the heart to tell her I'm not the slightest bit interested. "We're going virtual," says RUBy.

In her best storytelling voice she begins.

"Between 1914 and 1917, the explorer Sir Ernest Shackleton led the first expedition to cross Antarctica from sea to sea via the South Pole."

Suddenly, I am standing in a frozen wasteland. And for the next two hours, I experience what Shackleton and his crew endured for three long years.

I am there when Shackleton's ship, the *Endurance*, sinks in the icy waters off the coast of Antarctica. His crew stays behind on an ice floe while the captain and a few men go in life-boats for help. Both parties go through many hardships, but they never give up.

"Captain Shackleton took a few of his men in one lifeboat for a daring ride to the closest inhabited island with a town and radio in order to rescue the others. They had to sail to South Georgia Island, eight hundred miles away."

"No way," I say. "All they have to make the journey with is a stopwatch and the stars to guide them?" I am in the little lifeboat named the *James Caird*, when a hurricane hits. The boat is blown to shore with the men inside hanging on for dear life. Then we walk twenty miles to a town.

RUBy says, "It took four more months and four attempts to rescue the remaining twenty-two men Shackleton had left behind. That boat journey aboard the *James Caird* was a supreme act of human courage."

Nothing boring about the Shackleton story.

"Thank you, RUBy; that was some adventure. And to think the Shackleton party never quit."

PARTY

"Come," Rizin calls from his office door after I knock.

Everybody screams, "Happy birthday, Houston!"

I stand there looking like a piece of lint on a black shirt. Not sure how to take all this. I haven't had a birthday party since before Rizin became my guardian. He doesn't believe in such stuff. How in the world did they get him to go along with this?

Carlos must see the confusion on my face. I'm totally stunned. "Nobody pays much attention to a cyborg's birthday," I mumble. "Most of us don't even remember when we were truly born. The government measures our existence from the day we were made with our synthetic parts."

"Oh, nothing is impossible for RUBy to find," Carlos explains.

"True, true," I agree with a smile. "I wish she could be here with us," I add.

"But she is. Carlos has downloaded RUBy into an away computer."

The handheld computer screen glows pink. "Happy birthday, Houston!" RUBy giggles. It amazes me that this powerful machine *giggles*.

Leanna's smiling so big. "Rizin helped us with our plans. It was his idea to keep you occupied with the Shackleton story while we set up for the party."

I'm shocked. "Is that true?" I ask my uncle.

"I was outnumbered," he says. "They all wanted to pull this party together. Not my kind of thing, but it was a good way of getting you to learn about Captain Shackleton. Tell me, what did the story say to you?"

"Shackleton was a great leader who never gave up. His crew remained unified on that desolate ice floe and trusted that Shackleton would return. It was a together story."

"Nice!" Rizin says. "Here on the Moon we Moonborgs have a motto that comes from this story. *Courage defeats the impossible.* Keep it close."

All I can think to say is, "Hey, thanks. This is really frisk — completely cool."

"Try the cake," says Carlos. "The ship's base cook fixed it just for you."

I take a slice. It's red velvet cake, made with Saturn sugar, which is hot-sweet. Spicy and soothing at the same time. "Whoa, this is *good*."

Leanna can't stop smiling. Even though I've started eating, she pulls a birthday candle from her pocket. "We only found one candle in the whole city."

Rizin's into the cake now, eating as fast as me. "No need for candles," he scoffs.

RUBy says, "We know how old you are, Houston." Leanna puts the one candle on the side of the cake that hasn't been sliced. "Imagine there are seventeen candles when you blow this one out."

"Don't forget to make a wish." Carlos is bouncing from foot to foot. Typical kid at a birthday party.

"My wish is that we always stay friends," I say.

"*No!*" Carlos shouts. "You're not supposed to *tell* your wish."

"Oh, I forgot. It's been so long since I've had any kind of birthday anything. Sorry." I go for my second piece of cake. "Okay, so now you know what I want more than anything." But this is only half true. There's another wish brewing.

Everybody, even Rizin, sings "Happy Birthday." I blow out the one candle.

"Here's something for you," says Leanna.

She hands me a small package. I open it. Wow! A bag of Rock Poppers — the best candy in the universe.

"I love these," I say, opening the bag and offering them to everyone.

Carlos gives me a star chart. "I made it," he said. "You can attach it to your biofe eye and study the heavens. Just remember to look away from the Sun."

"You're okay, Carlos," I say, giving him a fake jab to the shoulder.

He gives me the signal for a cyborg thumb-thump. I thump his thumb, and he quickly touches my thumb with his own. Thumb-thump done right.

"Frisk," says Leanna. "Where'd you learn that?"

"RUBy researched it for me," Carlos answers. "I figure if I'm going to be around cyborgs, I'll need to know how to communicate."

"I wanna do it," says Leanna, repeating the thumb-thump with me.

RUBy's next with a gift for me. "Open it," she says.

I tear off the wrapping paper. It's an old copy of a magazine that was popular in the twentieth and early-twenty-first centuries, *Sports Illustrated*. The paper copies are hard to find now, since everything's virtual. Holding an actual magazine makes it so real. "This is *beyond* frisk," I say.

Carlos beams, looking all proud of himself. "It's not an actual antique copy. RUBy reproduced it from a historical copy. But it looks real, right?"

To hold a copy in my hand is as special as holding Joey Mercer's swifting glove. I look closely at the magazine and smile. "I can't wait to read this, front to back. Thanks, Leanna, Carlos, and RUBy."

FAMILIAR

Rizin pushes away from his desk and stands up. He looks taller, stronger, and fiercer than ever. "Although celebrating birthdays is not the cyborg way, I'm glad I allowed it," Rizin says. I know that if Li Rizin didn't want me to have a birthday party there wouldn't have been one.

Rizin slaps me on the shoulder, walks to the back of his chair, and stands there as if prepared to make an important announcement.

"Houston. You're now seventeen. Ordinarily, we cyborgs don't get our Familiars until we are eighteen." Rizin holds me in the gaze of his expressive eyes. "In the absence of your father, who was my best friend, I have the authority to make this call.

"Because of the mature way in which you protected and defended Leanna for The Liberty Bell Movement," Rizin continues, "and escaped with the prototype of an interplanetary spaceship, I think you are ready to receive your Familiar now."

This is the best gift ever! I'm getting my Familiar — at seventeen! I'm wearing a grin on my face that won't hold back.

"What's a Familiar?" Carlos asks.

"Yeah, and what's familiar about it?" Leanna adds.

I'm ready with the answer. "Years ago, it was decided that cyborgs would be sent to the Moon to work the mines. They were given locator chips so the Federation would know where they were at all times. But the Moon cyborgs, or Moonborgs, created an overriding system using the DNA of an animal. It confused the locator chip."

"Sorta like putting red pepper in the tracks of runaway slaves to confuse the hounds that were chasing them," says Leanna. "I learned that in All-Virtual School."

"Exactly. Our Familiars are part of us. We can project them as biographs, and we can use their strengths and powers to help us when we need help."

"What's going to be your Familiar?" Carlos asks.

"I like the lion," I explain. Rizin knows I've always loved that big cat. "But," I add, "your elder gets to choose." I hold my breath, waiting for Rizin's decision.

"I've chosen the wolf for you, Houston. Wolves are individually strong yet loyal to one another and loving toward the females and pups. It's a perfect match for you," Rizin says.

I want to lash out and say I think the wolf is *not* me! I hate the idea. But I fluff up and play the part of an obedient nephew. "I admire many of the wolf's qualities. I'd be honored to have it as my Familiar."

"Alpha wolf, no doubt!" says Leanna with a wink.

I turn back to Rizin, trying not to show my disappointment. "Uncle, can I get my biofe ear, too?" I know I'm pushing it.

"What's a biofe ear?" Leanna asks.

Rizin answers. "A biofe ear makes our hearing stronger, more intense. We can hear what the speaker is really meaning in spite of the words he or she uses. The biofe ear is a tool that can help us in uncertain situations, but an untrained cyborg can become overly suspicious and it can, in extreme cases, lead to madness. A Familiar is one thing, but a biofe ear is another matter."

Rizin's response to my request is simple and to the point. "No biofe ear." And the way he says it means no further discussion. I won't let it go, though.

"But according to tradition, getting the Familiar and the biofe ear happens at the same time. Why can't I have the ear for the same reason you say I'm ready to get my Familiar?"

"You have much more learning to do, Houston. More growing up. You're not fully ready for a biofe ear."

Rizin comes to me, lands both his big hands on my shoulders. "Save the dramatics for later," he says. "Familiar now, biofe ear later."

"But . . ."

Rizin's eyes narrow. There is no patience left in his voice. "Houston, the way you keep questioning my decision makes me wonder if you are even ready for your Familiar. Maybe you should wait until next year to get your wolf *and* biofe ear."

"Familiar now, biofe ear later," I say in submission. Rizin *always* gets what he wants.

The Sun is so hot. White.

It comes on strong, retreats, comes back, retreats again. But always burns against the blanket of black. I dare not look at the hot white. My emotions are all over the place. I'm happy because I'm getting my Familiar. But I'm searing mad at Rizin for denying me my biofe ear. What's the purpose? If I'm mature enough to get my Familiar, then why not my biofe ear? I don't buy that jazz about it taking more maturity to manage an ear than a Familiar. I think it's all about control, showing me who's in charge.

I keep my gaze to the ground as I move through Shackleton fast, pushing out my breath. Slicing through people to get where I'm going — getting madder and madder at Rizin.

I have watched Shackleton grow over the years. The domed city is open and spacious, much like its sister city, Atlantis, on Earth. It has open areas like parks, where you can see to the top of the dome. It even rains, which makes it feel so natural, like the soft drizzle that's falling now. So many people live in this bustling, busy city, doing things just like at home. In no time at all I reach the east tower building, where Epps's office is located.

I've known Epps forever. She's a cyborg doctor, but she won't answer to anything but Epps. All of her patients are cyborgs, but they are very different from the ones on Earth. Here on the Moon, they're called Moonborgs, because their artificial parts are sometimes very visible and radical. On Earth most of the cyborgs try to look as much like Firsts as possible. Like me.

Stepping into her waiting room, the automatic intercom system announces my visit. *"Epps, Houston Ye has arrived for his Familiar implant."*

I get nervous for the first time when the system says, *"Mr. Ye, the doctor will see you in a few moments; please have a seat."*

The man sitting next to me is a good example of a Moonborg. He has no mouth or nose. Another patient has no eye where one should be.

"What are you staring at, First? Get out of here before I pound you into dust!" A hostile Moonborg's four eyes swirl around like rolling marbles on top of little flagpoles sticking out of his shoulders.

"Hey," I say forcefully while holding my hand up in a battle-ready position. "Talk what you know. I *am* a cyborg!"

Before I can say anything more, Epps steps between us.

"So I see you have met Mr. Houston Ye, Rizin's nephew, who is very much a cyborg."

"Oh, I'm sorry, man," says Four-eyes. "I thought you was a First, for real. . . . Please, don't tell Mr. Rizin 'bout this."

"He won't," says Epps. "I'll be with you as soon as I'm fin-ished." Then Epps pushes me into the next room. "Get up on the examination table."

"I see you're happy this morning," I say sarcastically.

Epps is almost pretty and some might say petite. She's got no bedside manner and her 'tude is miserable. But she's always been my best ally and a good shoulder to lean on.

Epps turns away from me to pick up some of her medical supplies. "Rizin told me all about your response to the wolf. You hate it."

"I didn't tell him that," I answer.

"You forget he has a biofe ear. He *heard* what you really felt. Here — take off your shirt and lie back on your right side."

"I don't want a wolf for my Familiar. I've always admired the lion," I say.

"I know, but what do you know about the wolf?"

"I just don't like 'em."

"I hear a lot of anger and confusion in your words," Epps says quietly. "I hear you're saying that it is easier to be angry with the wolf than at your mother for abandoning you, right?"

"Right," I whisper. "I forget you have a biofe ear, too. Then you gotta know that if Mom hadn't pushed to get that last picture of a red wolf, we might not have had the accident."

"That picture helped keep the wolf from going extinct. Look. Placing blame is not the best way to overcome a tragedy. Peace comes with understanding and acceptance. What did your mother lose?"

I don't even try to answer. Epps keeps talking.

"Getting a Familiar of any breed and at age seventeen makes it even more special. I disagree with Rizin on the biofe ear. It's great to have when you're a cyborg trying to survive in a hostile world. Now, lie back so I can start. And stop looking like a scared puppy."

I lie down on my side and look at the monitor on the wall. I smile knowing that Epps has my back. She's always been an excellent ally, the only person I know who will stand up to Rizin without flinching.

Epps gives me an injection that paralyzes me from head to ankles. "We will communicate by using your feet," she says. "Wiggle your toes if the answer is yes. Keep still if the answer is no. Curl your toes under to show extreme pain. Understand?"

I wiggle my toes.

Her hand gracefully begins to draw on my neck and shoulder.

"We take a charcoal sketch of the wolf," she says, walking me through the procedure. "Like this wolf?" The monitor shows a perfect view of it. I wiggle my toes. The big alpha leader appears so real. So frisk.

"Rule number one." Epps begins my lesson on the care of my Familiar. "Don't abuse your wolf. They can die and it's hard to replace them."

I'm wondering all the while how a computer chip dies.

"Rule number two, your Familiar is your best friend and will do whatever you ask of it, so don't break rule number one. Wiggle your toes if you get it."

I wiggle both feet.

"Now I'm applying black and red liquid that looks like a regular tattoo, but it's really silica infused with nanomachine processors. The silica is the biograph projector, which allows your Familiar to appear to come to life. Inside the silica are tiny machines that manipulate gravity, light, and other stuff. They make it all work."

Then Epps inserts the wolf's DNA. Even though Epps has numbed me, this part of the procedure hurts down to my toes, which are now curled under. She quickly adds more pain relief.

"When you activate the wolf, the drawing will turn bright red. When it's off, it will be black, just as it is now. In a few minutes this will begin to hurt again as the silica binds to your skin and nervous system. The wolf gets its power from you, so you will feel drained when you use it. If you want to use the wolf a lot, you may have to get a power pack."

It's all over in about an hour. I am amazed at how easy it is, and there's not much pain after the DNA insertion. I walk over to the mirror on wobbly legs. The image of the wolf covers my lower neck and part of my shoulder. It's not a lion, but the wolf looks really better than I could have imagined. I tell Epps, "I'm gonna read up on the red wolf as soon as I get back."

Suddenly, Epps sits me up on the table. "While the systems boot up, I'm going to give you a biofe ear," says Epps, telling me to sit still.

"But Rizin said I wasn't supposed to get one. Why are you helping me?" I ask.

"Because you didn't ask me to do it. I would never defy an elder's orders because a kid wants me to. I'm overriding Rizin's decision based on a safety issue. Few can tell you're a cyborg. That could be trouble for you. You need a Familiar *and* a biofe ear for protection. You could be arrested or attacked by one of those crazy fanatics from the Bureau of Cyborg Affairs, who are out to oppress cyborgs and end the cyborg race. The biofe ear keeps young cyborgs safe. I've known you for years, Houston, and I think you're ready. Oh, and don't worry. Let me deal with Rizin."

Leave it to Epps to work it out for me. Epps uses a pair of tweezers to hold a very small disk, which she inserts in my ear. On the screen the disk grows eight leglike appendages that attach themselves to my eardrum and my nervous system.

I feel queasy. "Epps. What's it doing?"

She explains that it's a self-attaching biofe and that it will activate in a few hours or so. "When it kicks in, you will be hungry, so eat. Make your wolf happy."

Before I leave, Epps asks, "Everyone who gets a Familiar gives the Familiar a name. Have you thought of yours?"

Have I thought of mine? The real question is when have I *not* thought about naming my Familiar? From the time I knew what a Familiar was, I had the name of my lion picked out — Leopold. But it just doesn't fit a wolf.

Suddenly, a name leaps into my mouth. "Apache," I tell her.

"What!" I shout. Two of my favorite Moonborgs, Stick and Tools, are waiting for me when I leave Epps's office. We hug and slap each other's backs. They've been away mining in the South Fields all month, and now they're back for some rest.

"So we hear you got your Familiar. Now you are a true Moonborg, one of our family," says Stick.

Suddenly, I realize something. The biofe ear has kicked in. I'm able to hear the sounds between the spoken words — where the truth is found. Stick meant everything he said. I'm his family. I had no doubt that he was being truthful, but it feels wonderful having it confirmed by my biofe ear.

I've known Stick and Tools since I was a kid visiting the Moon during summer break. They were my babysitters, my friends, though they aren't like any other cyborgs I've ever known.

Tools got his name because he has so many biofe parts he looks like a bag of tools. While working in a chemical plant, he accidentally put his hands in a container of acid.

Tools once explained it to me this way: "Instead of replacing them with regular hands, I got tools attached that can be useful in any work."

I always thought the idea was frisk. Still do.

Now, Stick is another matter. He has a biofe mouth. But it isn't in the place where the mouth is usually located. Stick put his biofe mouth in the palm of his left hand. Honest. He raises his hand to say hello to me.

Epps is so right. Moonborgs are not afraid of being who they are. They don't think of themselves as freaks. Here they're individuals.

"Getting your Familiar calls for a celebration," Tools says. So we go off to find something fun. A perfect way to avoid confronting Rizin about my ear.

THE PEACE OFFERING

I'm in Rizin's office. He's the maddest I've ever seen him. "I told you not to get a biofe ear. Why did you go behind my back?"

"I didn't ask for it," I answer. "Dr. Epps used her medical authority to override your command. She felt I needed the ear for safety," I say, shrugging.

"A pox on that woman!" Rizin shouts.

I tell Leanna when I come back from Rizin's office, "I don't know why Rizin is so off the bridge about a biofe ear."

"No reason to be angry with Rizin. You should have known he wasn't going to let you off easy when you defied him," says Leanna.

I feel the need to talk to RUBy.

"Are you there? RUBy, you're aware of what's been going on. What can I do?"

"You must find a way to fix it," RUBy answers. Her screen flashes orange. "Earn Rizin's trust again."

"You mean get rid of the ear?" I ask, half knowing that I really don't want to do that.

"No," RUBy says. "I've got a better plan."

RUBy has a plan? An independently devised plan? No way! Either she's some kind of a new Artificial Intelligence that can think, or she's something else.

RUBy goes on. "All military and governmental AI systems are in one way or another connected." The computer displays the entire worldwide comm grid.

"But they have firewalls, data defense servers, and tracking," I put in.

RUBy has a quick answer. "The defense system is designed for AI's and others who are not authorized. I remain authorized because Dr. Pace wants all communication lines open, in case Carlos tries to contact him."

I try to hear RUBy's words. Nothing. Blank. The ear doesn't work with her. "What are you going to do?"

"I'm going to hack into the chancellor's personal files and see what we can find. You can give it to Rizin as a peace offering."

RUBy's colors change three or four times. When she speaks again, she is red, happy because she has a million triggabits of data. She's sucked up the content of a library in less than five seconds.

I rush to Rizin's office. He's there with Epps. I come in on an argument between them about my biofe ear. "You helped the boy betray me," Rizin is saying.

"I *helped* the boy stay safe," Epps defends.

They both look startled when they see me standing there.

Rizin says, "There's nothing that can be done now. The biofe ear is in. I must accept this, Epps. But know that I'm not pleased about it."

I stop the argument by saying, "Sir, use your biofe eye to connect with RUBy's systems. Then watch the diary log from Chancellor Graham's office. It's about the aliens called The O," I explain. "Seems they paid him a visit, too."

Rizin reads.

//WFN/Chancellor/Personal
Date: December 6, 2170
Earth Time: 10:34:34 pm PT

At the WFN headquarters in Troy, the twin biosphere to Atlantis, located off the coast of Santiago, Chile, Taylor Graham stands at the tower window while staring into the blue ocean below and contemplating his next move. Behind him hangs the WFN flag — the one he has just sworn to defend as the newly elected chancellor.

Suddenly, two humanoids materialize behind him. Graham, who was the former Secretary of Planetary Security, instinctively braces for the worst.

"Is this an invasion, an attack?" the chancellor asks.

"We mean you no harm," say the visitors. "We are The O, and we've come in peace with a warning and a message. We know of your plans to venture into deep space. But your world is not ready."

Chancellor Graham raises an eyebrow. "I beg to differ with you, sirs. Our world is a far better place than it was a hundred years ago," he says proudly. "We haven't had a war in over fifty years. Nations have worked together to conquer many diseases so people are living longer and better in safer and healthier environments. We live in peace and promote good-will among the peoples of the world."

"We have noted human progress, but there are other weak-nesses that persist, and we cannot overlook them at this time. Be warned. If you launch your space program we will stop you," The O say.

"Your ultimatum seems to come straight from the plot of an old twentieth-century sci-fi novel — a bad one at that. You act as if we humans don't value freedom, justice, and peace."

"You humans cherish the idea of liberty, but humans fall short when it comes to practicing it."

"What are you talking about? Who are we oppressing?" Chancellor Graham throws up his arms in disgust. "You sound like that Liberty Bell gang, spinning the absurd notion that clones should be free." Graham laughs, but he stops when he realizes that The O don't find the idea as ridiculous as he does.

The O move into the light, where the chancellor can get a very good look. Graham gasps and immediately reaches into his desk for a weapon. "Security!" he yells.

The O twist the chancellor's vibogun into a ball of metal with one glance. Then The O step back into the shadows. "You are not ready to meet all the new species you will encounter. Will you kill us all because we are different?"

Graham is too startled to answer.

"Different is not a synonym for wrong," The O continue. "And know this. They are not rocks."

"Yes, yes, yes, you have issued the warning 'they are not rocks' many times, and we are still discovering the true meaning of this phrase," Graham scoffs, adding, "During my campaign, I promised the people of Earth that as the Chancellor of The World Federation of Nations I will lead them into a new space age. I plan to do that, and I won't let you stop us."

The chancellor's security team bursts through the office door, viboguns drawn. But The O have already disappeared.

THE T

"RUBy, you were right!" Rizin is so impressed that we got the information about The O.

I tell RUBy, "The chancellor's made alien boogeymen out of The O, and they don't seem to be saying anything more than 'clean up your act.'"

"Did he forgive you for getting a biofe ear?" she asks, glowing a neon pink.

"I think all is well."

"That's great. You did just fine!"

"RUBy, it was all your idea. I did nothing but deliver the download. Which brings me to a question I have. I've been watching you and trying to figure out what you are. You're posing as a computer, but you're not like any computer I know about. So who are you? *What* are you?"

There's a long pause. Then RUBy answers. "I'd like to think that I am your friend. Friends don't question friends."

Later, I meet Carlos in the lounge and we flip on the T. To our surprise, Taylor Graham, the High Chancellor of The World

Federation of Nations, is on full screen, ranting about The Liberty Bell teaming up with The O to take over the world.

"*We have two of the leaders of the subversive organization known as The Liberty Bell in custody and we have their full confessions. By their own independent admissions, The Liberty Bell organization takes orders from aliens known as The O. And The O are determined to stop Earth from advancing in outer space trade and exploration. They want to keep us captive on Earth. They've gotten members of The Liberty Bell to cap-ture our prototype space vessel and they've kidnapped Dr. Marcus's son, Carlos. No telling what they have done with that poor child.*"

At this point, Chancellor Graham turns aside as if reacting to the horror of what might be happening to Carlos.

Meanwhile, Carlos is as gray as RUBy. "What? He doesn't know what he's talking about. I'm fine and nobody has hurt me!"

"And nobody stole me!" says RUBy. "I brought you here because I refused to be a part of the program that depended on —"

"Okay, RUBy," Carlos says, stopping her from completing her thought. But my biofe ear hears *secret, caution, say no more.*

What are these two hiding? What is their secret? I decide not to probe or let on that I suspect anything. "He's trying to drum up support for his own plans," I say.

Graham continues. "*Several of the traitors are on the Moon, and we are dispatching Joe Spiller of the Clone Humane Society to bring them back for trial.*"

RUBy's light turns white. "He is lying about The O."

Chancellor Graham sighs deeply. "*We need to be careful during these critical times. We suspect there is an underground movement that is being supported by cyborgs and their friends. We are watching them.*"

Hanging out here in Shackleton is the most fun I've had in a long time, but now that I've got a biofe ear, I've heard loneliness in Leanna's and Carlos's voices, and more than a little pain. So I decide to do what I can to cheer them up whenever I can.

Rizin signals that he wants all three of us to come to the operation center.

The main operations center for the Moon biosphere is deep in the Shackleton Crater.

The elevator tube opens to a vast room with a holograph table showing the biosphere's control center. There sits a big green-eyed Irishman with a head full of unruly red hair. His voice is coarse as is his dress. He is not a cyborg, but he's not like any First I've ever seen. Governor Big House may not have biofe parts, but he's got the swagger, the mannerisms, and the language of a true cyborg. To me he's a very likable person . . . for a First.

As soon as we are seated, the governor begins. "Listen up — the high chancellor will be addressing the nations in a few minutes. We have all been ordered to view it."

The lights dim and a holographic image of Graham walks to a podium. I can feel the tension in the room.

"Greetings to all of you," Chancellor Graham says. He is standing straight and tall and his voice is the sound of authority. There is no doubt about who's in charge.

"Today marks the beginning of the next great human endeavor. As I promised during my campaign, we will launch a fleet of ships to explore the stars. This will be the greatest adventure we have ever undertaken.

"Before we can make the step into deep space, we must first ensure that our home is safe and secure. We have solved poverty. We have solved world hunger. We have even stopped warring."

The holograph changes the view to include the small audience of people in the room with the chancellor. It appears to be full of dignitaries from around the world. I recognize a few of them, like the presidents of Ghana, China, the United States, Russia, and Argentina. They clap politely in support of the comment about stopping wars.

"We have one cancerous problem left that started small and now has become a true danger to us all. It began when people tried to prolong life. People got transplants, then cloned parts and biofe parts." The chancellor shakes his head. "Some people even killed to steal the parts of innocent people. Shameful behavior. Inhumane." The dignitaries nod in agreement.

"Innocently, we thought we were helping people by giving them biofe hearts and kidneys as replacements. Biofe legs to help people walk again. Biofe eyes to help people see again. Then it happened. Next, people replaced perfectly good legs and eyes so they could compete better in sports. Or stay younger. Our humanity was at risk. Laws were passed to protect us from these abominations against nature."

The audience stands up and applauds loudly. Taylor Graham waves his hands to tell them to settle down so he can finish his announcement. I can't believe what I'm hearing.

"Now we have cyborgs mixing their bodies with animal DNA tattoos. They call them Familiars. How soon will it be before our children will want them?"

I feel self-conscious. This speech isn't sitting well with me or any of the cyborgs in the room. The command center is completely silent.

The chancellor moves from behind the podium and paces back and forth as he talks. "The Wholers, a group of people loyal to this planet, decided to do something about this disease among us. The Wholers are a group that I proudly support because of their work to preserve the greatness of humankind. Today, we ensured that our humanity will be protected from the excesses of this world, from the corruption of those who would confuse and mutilate our children.

"The Wholer Act was made law today." Everyone in the room with the chancellor cheers loudly. The chancellor returns to the podium. The cheering stops so he can continue. "The simple law wants all of us to be whole. To be human, just as we are when we are born. Not mixed with animal DNA or plastic parts. The World Federation of Nations has voted to change the old three-fifths law defining cyborgs. Any person who has a biofe part of any kind is now a cyborg. This will deter our children from mutilating their bodies and becoming freaks of nature."

The room in which the chancellor is speaking erupts in strong steady applause. After a while the noise dies down.

"Now, we know there is a movement to protest this new definition. We will not tolerate any civil disobedience. We will not be intimidated by lawless tactics. The law is the law. Accept it."

There is silence. "Thank you for your attention. Thank you for your support. And thank you for being supporters of the Wholers."

Taylor Graham finishes his announcement. The transmission ends.

Everyone in the command center is stunned by what the chancellor has said.

Slowly, Big House stands up to address us. "Well, people, I've never heard a speech like that before. As you know, I've always wanted to be a cyborg. Do I get my biofe ear now, Mr. Rizin?" the governor says, joking with Rizin, who is standing next to him.

"I always knew you were a wannabe cyborg," Rizin says, continuing the joke. But according to Graham, Big House is now a cyborg because he has a biofe heart.

Leanna wants answers. "Rizin, I heard what the chancellor said, but I really don't understand what this means."

Rizin's face saddens for just a moment, then he answers. "The chancellor will start removing leaders worldwide and replacing them with his own friends. More important, Governor Big House can be removed from office because cyborgs are not allowed to be governors."

Big House speaks to Rizin, Carlos, Leanna, and me. "You know the chancellor is going to call in a few minutes. I'm sure he's going to ask for my resignation. And he's going to order your arrest for treason."

"We will fight him," one of the men standing at his station says. The others in the room start to murmur in agreement.

"Governor, sir," one of the station officers says. "The chancellor's office is calling for you." Rizin looks at Big House. They both smile knowingly at each other. Then Big House nods to the communication officer that he will take the call where he is standing.

The center holograph activates and the image of Taylor Graham appears. Big House immediately calls everyone to order. Everyone in the room sits and faces the holographic image.

"Good evening, Chancellor." The governor speaks politely.

"Let's dispense with the pleasantries, Governor. I'm relieving you of your office according to the Cyborg Act, which says cyborgs may not hold any public office," the chancellor barks at Big House.

"Yes, I know that law well. But I'm not a cyborg. I'm a First," the governor snaps back.

"No, you're not, according to the Wholer Act, passed earlier today. Your biofe heart makes you a cyborg." Taylor Graham counters like a tennis player by hitting the ball back into the governor's court.

"Not so fast, Chancellor. I'm ordering my personal doctor to remove my biofe heart. I will just have to wait until a donor heart becomes available. Anyway, I remain a First and Governor of the Moon Base."

"Where are you going to get one? You know it's illegal to buy a heart or even get one cloned. You have five days to get a biological heart. Make it easy. Just accept that you're a cyborg. Resign, Governor. Now!"

The chancellor's face is stern and full of anger at Big House. Suddenly, Rizin steps forward, glaring at the chancellor. "Sir, I'm already a cyborg. You can have my real heart."

"No, I'd be honored if he took mine, sir," a young guard says as he steps from behind his station. Everyone in the room who has a natural heart says they will exchange hearts with Big House to keep him a First and thus Governor of the Moon Base.

You'd think the chancellor would want men on his team who were so loved and respected by workers.

Taylor Graham's face reddens with anger and embarrass-ment. The Moon base soldiers have made it clear to him that they are on the governor's side.

"Well, Chancellor, I guess you see I have a heart," Big House says coldly.

In the very next moment, Chancellor Graham calms down. All traces of anger disappear. "There are other more impor-tant matters. You are harboring fugitives. The courts have demanded the return of Leanna Deberry for immediate exam-ination. You are holding a minor, Carlos Pace. You are helping a thief, Houston Ye, who stole government property. And finally, Governor, you are allowing a ruthless, heartless cyborg to orchestrate all of this — the outlaw cyborg Rizin. Therefore, I order you, Governor, to arrest the fugitives and turn them over to Joe Spiller immediately. He will be arriving at the Moon base within the next few hours. Then I will think about what to do with you."

The governor raises his right hand and snaps his fingers. The guards stationed in the corners of the room immediately surround us. "Sorry, old friend," Big House says to Rizin. "You are under arrest. Take them to the brig."

I touch the side of my neck and shoulder. My wolf feels hot. I can feel his heart beating simultaneously with my own. I say his name, Apache. Suddenly, I feel stronger, fiercer, and less frightened than I ever have before.

Apache appears next to me. He is a magnificent black and reddish-brown wolf with flame-yellow eyes and a tail that is pointed in attack mode. I feel strangely safe to hear him growling softly, and I feel him saying he is with me, no matter what.

A guard grabs for me. I watch in amazement as Apache attacks the man by disarming him. Afraid Apache might do more damage, I tap my shoulder to bring him home. The wolf springs at my shoulder and vanishes into the tattoo.

Everyone in the room is stunned except for Rizin. Using his biofe arms and legs, he scoops up Leanna, Carlos, and me like little toys and runs. Before I know it, we land on the floor of the elevator and the doors are closing.

"Did . . . did you see my wolf? Is he about the most wonderful thing you've ever seen?"

"I thought you hated the wolf —" Leanna scoffs.

"We don't have much time," Rizin points out, interrupting her. "We're a long way from RUBy. I hope we can make it."

Carlos tells RUBy we are on our way. "When the elevator stops, we start running. Don't turn around. Just run straight to RUBy." Rizin snaps the order.

He doesn't stop to take a breath. He is in battle-command mode. "Houston," he says urgently, "when the elevator stops, activate your wolf and be ready for an attack. Carlos, you run with Leanna!"

"Tools, Stick, Epps," Rizin calls to his partners. "We have a Code One. We need to protect Leanna. Get to the ship. Track us."

"Code One activated," comes a response from all three.

Carlos says to me, "Your wolf turned bright red and a flash of light jumped out from the side of your neck. That was frisk to the tenth power!"

The elevator comes to a bouncing halt and the door opens. As I was told, I activate Apache by tapping my shoulder. Rizin and I, with the help of my Familiar, easily disarm the guards, knocking them to the ground and leaving them unconscious.

Leanna and Carlos are ahead of us, running as fast as they can. To my horror, I can see more guards moving in. "Rizin, they're going to get caught!" I yell.

But from out of nowhere, Tools and Stick join the fight. The guards are no match for them, either. Tools smashes the guards' viboguns like cheap toys. We reach the street level and run to the hangar bay. The way looks clear. Then a viboblast flies past me and hits a nearby wall. "They're behind you," Leanna calls.

Epps opens the hangar doors. Guards close in. I order Apache to pounce. He leaps forward, teeth bared. I punch one guard out, and Apache bites the vibogun of another one. Epps fights the guards blocking the way to RUBy.

Leanna and Carlos make it to the ship first. Then me. Rizin and his crew bring up the rear. When I reach the ship, I deactivate my Familiar. "Great work," I tell Apache. I feel a little twitch in my shoulder. How could I have ever wanted anything but a wolf?

RUBy is powered up and ready for launch.

"Some friend you have in Governor Big House," Carlos says to Rizin. "You offer him your heart and he arrests you!"

"Hush!" Rizin barks at Carlos. "RUBy, connect me to the governor now."

Big House immediately asks, "Got everybody?"

"Yep," Rizin answers. "Are we on a secure comm?"

"You bet," says Big House. "The very one we designed together."

"Great."

"Okay. We are tracking Joe Spiller's ship now. RUBy needs to launch using vector eight-seven-six. Go as fast as you can straight at Spiller's ship. We will fire a few laser blasts at you to make this look real. Then we will *accidentally* hit Spiller's ship, which will disable it. Good luck. You are cleared for immediate launch. Go!"

"Thank you, my friend," Rizin returns.

RUBy launches without receiving orders from Rizin or Carlos. Another independent act. Interesting. The ship engages its main engines, zooming past Spiller's crippled ship sent to get us. We are heading back to Earth!

But right now, I really need to feed my wolf. I'm so hungry.

PART THREE
A CALL FOR JUSTICE

CHAMELEON

In less than four hours, RUBy announces that she is preparing for landing. "We are within Earth's gravitational pull. Take your seats and buckle up," she says. I notice that her screen is a forest green.

"That's her battle-ready glow," Carlos tells us. "First stop, Cyborg City."

Leanna and I rush to see out. "There's the blue marble," Leanna says. "I really miss my family and friends, but it's good to see the green trees and blue oceans of Earth. Did I tell you Sandra and I have been friends ever since we started kindergarten together? She has always stood by me, no matter what."

"Cool," I say.

"When Sandra found out that Mom was part of The Liberty Bell Movement and that I was a clone, she got a little bit weird about it at first but then came around. She's my ace, my girl."

"Hey, it's good to have an ace. And it's good to have so many people in your corner. I bet they miss you, too," I say.

"Time for us to get off," says Rizin. We'd already decided on a game plan for our escape. Rizin recaps so we're all in the same planning mode. "I've got some business to take care of," he says. "All of you go to Leanna's house; break her mom — Annette — and Dr. Ayala out of house arrest. Eventually, we'll all head for Mars, where we'll hide out among the spaceship builders who developed RUBy."

"Not to worry about us," says Tools. "We're getting ready to jumpstart these protests."

"We've heard about a meeting with Gray Davis, a young man who was just dismissed from Georgia Tech because it was discovered that he has two biofe replacements. We're going there to be part of the protest," Epps explains.

Leanna takes my hand. She's nervous. I can feel her trembling beside me.

"Don't get separated," says Rizin, getting up to board the city. "Houston, you know what to do. You have your Familiar now and your biofe ear. Put them to good use — protect and defend."

"Protect and defend," I repeat, saluting. Rizin and the others get off the ship.

Suddenly, Dr. Pace, Carlos's dad, comes on to RUBy's screen. "Carlos, this is your father. You stay right where you are until I get there!"

Dr. Pace has found a way to track the ship and tap into the communication system.

"I can't, Dad." Carlos sounds conflicted. He wants to obey his father. As far as I can tell, he *respects* his old man, but he doesn't *trust* his father when it comes to RUBy. Dr. Pace never liked the fact that Carlos decided to befriend RUBy and go off with her on his own.

My ear can hear this conflict loudly.

"Don't tell me what you can't do," Dr. Pace scolds. "RUBy is a one-of-a-kind spaceship, capable of doing incredible things. But in the wrong hands it could be used to do great harm to our homelands. Son, the ship is not a toy or a friend."

"That's where you're wrong, Dad," Carlos argues. "RUBy *is* my friend, and you know as well as I do how special she is. She doesn't want to hurt anyone."

"How dare you oppose me this way," says Dr. Pace. "I'm your father, and you will do as I say — now!"

Carlos chooses not to say more to his dad. It's like he's ignoring him. He tells us, "I can avoid detection for a while, but we have to keep moving. Stand ready, RUBy," Carlos says.

RUBy hasn't quieted her engines from the landing at Cyborg City when she begins her launch sequence — and we are off again.

We go to Leanna's place, where her mother, Annette Deberry, and her family's friend Dr. Anatol Ayala remain under house arrest.

Leanna and I are still holding hands. She usually seems older than thirteen. She's a tough girl, able to take care of herself in any situation. But lately, Leanna's seemed a little bit like a lost kid.

RUBy slows to a hover.

"Initiate chameleon mode," Carlos says.

"In progress," RUBy answers.

Carlos explains that RUBy can camouflage the ship by blending into the environment.

I've heard about this on T programs about spaceship capability. "Is it an invisibility device?" I ask.

"No," says Carlos. "Although RUBy appears to disappear altogether, she actually blends so well, she's not visible, even when she's in plain view."

RUBy comes to a stop in the park area across from Leanna's house, where we wait a few minutes before nightfall.

MOM

While we wait, Leanna talks about her mom. She speaks so lovingly. "My mom is everything to me. When my dad died, and it was just Mom and me, it was real hard. But Doc Doc, who's been our family doctor since I was a little girl, has kind of been like a grandfather to me."

My biofe ear tells me Leanna's got some real love going on for her mom and for Dr. Ayala, who she affectionately calls Doc Doc. *Sweet*, my ear says.

"Mom gives me the best hugs." Leanna's lost in a memory. "We had a three-hug promise. Mom promised me that no matter what, we'd hug three times every day. Mom always said that if we hugged once in the morning, again in the afternoon, then at night, the world would always seem like a good place." Leanna starts to cry softly. "I miss those hugs."

I'm listening and envying Leanna for the love she shares with her mom. All these years I've longed for a real family — for hugs and promises. And I've always wanted a mom who would love me — even as a cyborg.

But that's not the hand I was dealt. I'll be a cyborg forever, unloved by my mother — a throwaway. An *abomination*. I try not to focus on these kinds of thoughts, but when I hear Leanna talk, I can't help it. "You'll be getting a hug from your mom soon," I tell Leanna as we head for her house under the cover of darkness.

SANDRA

"The last time I was here," says Leanna, "I was running from Joe Spiller and those horrible biobots."

"You're lucky to be alive," I say.

Leanna moves carefully around the side of her house. There are no lights on inside. "This is the window I climbed out of." She tries to lift it, but she's afraid it will set off their alarm.

"Leanna Deberry? Is that you?" says someone approaching us. I get ready for an attack, but Leanna runs toward the person.

"Sandra! It's me." Leanna hugs a girl who steps from the shadows. They hop around in a silly dance of giggles and tears.

"I'm so glad to see you," says Sandra. "I've been worried sick. Where have you been?"

"Where's Mom?" Leanna asks. There was urgency in her voice.

"She's at Dr. Ayala's house. The authorities have allowed her to stay there because they think it would be easier to watch them together rather than separately."

"But she's okay? They haven't hurt her, right?"

"Far as I know, your mom and Dr. Ayala are fine. Just in custody of The WFN for activity with The Liberty Bell Movement." Sandra is looking at me, puzzled.

"Oh, this is my good friend Houston Ye," Leanna introduces me. Sandra just stares at me.

Good friend? Is that what Leanna thinks of me? I never would have expected her to use those words, but my biofe ear tells me that she is being sincere. Wow!

Sandra pulls Leanna to the side. Meanwhile, I am looking around, using my biofe eye to see possible danger. I check in with Carlos and RUBy. "Leanna's mom is not here," I say.

Carlos answers. "Wherever she is, we need to get going. RUBy can only hold the chameleon mode that keeps us from being tracked for a few more minutes. We need to get moving."

Thank goodness Sandra is a true friend. All the way real. No deceit. No hidden designs. Great!

"We're thinking about joining the protests against the Federation's Wholer Act," Leanna says.

"Seven kids from All-Virtual School are planning to pro-test also. Several students have been dismissed from school because they have one — just one — biofe part. That seems so unfair."

"The Wholers are radical," Leanna puts in.

"I'll rally up all the support we can from All-Virtual School. Don't worry. You aren't alone."

"Houston!" Carlos urges me to get back to the ship.

I start toward the spaceship and call over my shoulder for Leanna to follow quickly. The girls hug again. "You must go!"

Sandra pushes Leanna away. I can hear concern in her words.

As soon as we get on board, RUBy lifts off. Within seconds we land in the woods on the side of Dr. Ayala's mansion.

"I only have power enough to stay in chameleon mode for about thirty minutes," says RUBy.

"Give us an hour," I plead.

"Forty-five minutes, max!"

Leanna quickly leads me to a garage where we slip through a trapdoor and go down hidden stairs to a tunnel. Leanna seems to know where everything is located. I follow without question.

"I was here before," she whispers, "when I was running from Joe Spiller. This tunnel connects with Doc Doc's house. I stayed in the secret apartment over the garage. That's where Captain Newton of the Gypsy City came to get me dressed as #9767."

The tunnel gets tighter and darker. But we inch our way to the other end, climbing another set of stairs, then another set, until we are at Dr. Ayala's kitchen.

When Leanna and her mother meet, it is the same as with Sandra, but more intense. They hold each other tightly. Annette strokes her daughter's short hair and gently touches her face as if to prove to herself that Leanna is real and not a biograph.

I look away. This is such a private moment for mother and daughter. To my ear the few words they manage to say sound like a love song. For a brief moment I let myself think about my mother, Vickie Ye. I couldn't remember the last time I'd said her name. Then I blink her image away. This is too wonderful to ruin with negative thoughts.

"I am so, so glad to see you, Mom," says Leanna. "You look much better than you did at the preliminary trial. They'd used a mind probe. And I've been worried sick that it'd damaged your brain."

"All that's over now. The point is, how are you?"

I hear Annette holding back all the pain and hurt she's been through.

When things settle down, we realize that there is a virtual meeting in progress in Dr. Ayala's study. I am introduced to Supreme Court Chief Justice John Granbury. "Hello, sir," I speak, not sure whether I should bow or salute.

"Yes, yes, young people. We owe you a debt of gratitude, Houston, for keeping Leanna safe."

"Yes, sir," I say, pulling myself tall. This is the chief justice of the Supreme Court who is complimenting me.

"I always thought you were on our side," says Leanna, smiling.

"Yes, my father was a member of The Liberty Bell, and his father before him," says Chief Justice Granbury. "And I understand that you are our Custodian."

I'm hearing something that doesn't square with the chief justice's words. Not quite right. What?!

Leanna shakes her head and sighs. "Yes, Chief Justice, but I'm not so sure I know what that means."

"It's a big job, but from what Dr. Ayala tells me, you're up to it."

The sound I hear is like static, white noise. But it's gone now. The biofe ear must need an adjustment.

"You remember Lyle Adams, our defense lawyer, don't you?" says Doc Doc.

"Of course." Leanna responds with a squeeze of her mother's hand and a quick smile.

Adams skips all the formalities and goes legal.

"The Federation Supreme Court will not allow Leanna to be used as evidence in Ayala and Annette's treason case unless they can examine her," he says to the group.

Adams is uncertain. I'm not hearing the commitment a defense attorney should have for such·an important case. This makes me wonder. If they are represented by this guy, they don't have a duck's chance in a fox's court.

"Right now, the Federation High Court is refusing to hear the case because Attorney General Thompson is arguing that Leanna's a hoax. As I suggested at the preliminary trial, if you turn Leanna over to me, then she can be tested under my protection. Once they prove she is a clone and not a hoax, then I'd have a stronger argument."

I don't like that idea. The last thing Rizin said to us was don't get separated.

"I don't want Leanna in the hands of the Federation," says Annette. "No way!"

I nod in agreement.

Adams throws me an eye dart. "Listen, it isn't really a bad idea," he says.

"Well, I think it is a crazy idea," I blurt out.

"And by whose authority do you jump in?" Adams jabs.

"Mine!" both Annette and Leanna say at the same time.

I stand taller.

"We need a victory right now. It might be a smart move to go in for testing," Doc Doc tries to reason.

"I don't know right now," Leanna says. "I need to think about it. I believe Chief Justice Granbury would do everything to keep me safe."

I don't like where she is going.

Leanna continues. "But I know Joe Spiller and the Clone Humane Society would do anything to capture me and then feed me to his biobots."

Now she's thinking.

"What an imagination!" says Adams.

"Well, you think about it," Chief Justice Granbury says rather matter-of-factly. "But I need to know your decision by the end of the week so that I can petition the court with new facts to consider."

There it is again. The noise.

Adams and Granbury check out of virtual.

I know Granbury is hiding something. Leanna can't go with this man. I don't care if he is the chief justice and claims to be part of The Liberty Bell.

"Houston, this is Carlos. I think we've been found. We've got to go now!"

Annette and Dr. Ayala quickly show their support.

"Go, Leanna. Stay safe," pleads Annette.

"Without you, our hard work, our hopes and dreams, will have been for nothing," says Doc Doc.

"But we came to get you two," Leanna resists.

"We can't go now!" says Annette. "The chancellor has shot himself in the foot by pushing the passage of the Wholer Act. He's made allies out of people who ordinarily wouldn't speak. And they are rallying all over the world in protest. We've got to strike while everyone is fired up. Our people need us."

"The Liberty Bell needs you," says Doc Doc. "You are our Custodian now, so they will look to you for leadership."

"Lead them to do what?"

"That is up to you."

Leanna told me Dr. Ayala had taken care of her for as long as she can remember. She respects him and loves him without reservation, so what Doc Doc is saying reaches Leanna's core.

"I — I'll try my best to be a good Custodian."

"And I promise to help her," I say, shaking Doc Doc's hand.

Annette hugs me and whispers, "She can be stubborn sometimes."

Don't I know that to be true.

"But," Annette adds, "please take care of my child."

"I need you to come now," Carlos calls.

We rush through the tunnel to the garage and out the trap-door. RUBy is in full view, a sitting duck. Leanna and I scramble for the door and fall onto the main deck.

Carlos has RUBy ready to launch as soon as we get on board. Within minutes we are soaring high above the hemisphere. As soon as we are outside Earth's gravitational pull, RUBy levels off.

"It's harder to track us here. RUBy's metals are so new, she's not easily detectable by Federation security systems," explains Carlos. "Yet I can get you anywhere you need to go in minutes, let you off, and hide out up here until I'm needed again."

Leanna is impressed. They do a thumb-thump. "You are our boy genius."

"This is perfect," I say, clapping my hands like a coach trying to keep his swifters spirited. "Okay. We need to go to Cyborg City, where we can check in with our crew."

After a quick meal and a twenty-minute kick back, RUBy drops us off at Cyborg City.

"What's happening, cuteness?" Epps says. She's teasing and she knows I know it, so her flirting doesn't count.

"Epps, I need you to look at my biofe ear. I've been getting a lot of static," I say.

Epps frowns before she says anything. "Static is a reading. Better listen," she warns.

Tools looks concerned about something. One look at Stick and I understand what's going on. Stick's mouth-hand is all bandaged. "He got into it with security guards who were looking for Rizin," explains Tools. "As soon as a guard sees that we are cyborgs, he tries to mess with us, so Stick slaps the brute. The marshal monkey grabs Stick's mouth and tries to rip it out of his hand. Stick bites the scoundrel to make him let go. But Stick gets hurt in the fight. Now he's all bandaged up."

Tools says, "Hello — have you read the Cyborg Act lately? It's illegal for us to hold public demonstrations. If we protest, there's gonna be violence."

Stick says, "We don't have much of a chance against the Federation, but I'd die trying."

Rizin asks all of us, "What's our motto?"

We all say together, "Courage defeats the impossible."

"I say let them try to stop us. We'll show them cyborgs aren't easily shoved around," says Tools. "I can throw down anybody who gets in my way and hammer them good."

IN NEED OF A PLAN

There's distress on Leanna's face. Her shoulders are tensed.

Rizin has noticed Leanna, too. "You got something to say, Leanna?"

"I was thinking that we might wanna take up the non-violent approach to civil disobedience used by the Reverend Dr. Martin Luther King, Jr., during the Civil Rights Movement. We learned about it at school last year. Peaceful protest was Dr. King's way of dealing with discrimination during the twenti-eth century."

Tools says, "Yeah, yeah — I know all about Dr. King's stuff. He's the peace man people are always quoting when they've pounded you into dust, but when you stand up to fight, they suddenly start talking about peace."

"That just seems stupid to me," Stick says.

"How about *no* peace?" Tools spits in disgust.

Leanna is thinking. So is Rizin.

I say, "I know you guys are cool about being cyborgs, but *come on*. Haven't you had enough of being treated like animals? Aren't you sick of being Seconds and having no rights?"

"You sound like Gray Davis, the cyborg dude who was kicked out of that big engineering school in Georgia," says Stick.

"You know what I think?" says Tools. "That kid didn't care if we helped him or not. He's a cyborg, but he doesn't like cyborgs. He got what he deserves."

Now Leanna has become uncommonly quiet. I nudge her softly. She nods. "I studied Dr. Martin Luther King, Jr., and the Civil Rights Movement of the 1960s. He accomplished a lot without having to use violence. We might try the nonviolent approach. It will take courage to make it happen."

"Let's hear more," says Epps.

"Dr. King is one of the many historical biographs I have stored in my commglasses," Leanna explains. They are like sunglasses but better. Commglasses allow anyone who wears them to enter a virtual world — to actually travel back in time. To *be* there, *at* events.

Leanna gives us the lowdown. "Dr. Ayala designed my commglasses program so I'd have the wisdom and experiences of great historical figures who could help me make decisions and solve problems," she tells us. "The glasses are *the* coolest accessory a girl can have."

Leanna uses her glasses to bring Dr. King's biograph into the room. Cyborgs gather to get a good look.

"How may I help you, Leanna?" Dr. King says.

"I'm trying to convince these cyborgs that their protest might have better success if they use a nonviolent approach. Would you help explain it?"

Dr. King is standing before us in his best Sunday church suit, with a perfectly starched white shirt and cuff links.

He's shorter than I imagined, but I'm totally awed by this man.

"Rizin, good to meet you," Dr. King says. "Leanna has told me a lot about you."

Dr. King's voice is so powerful. We all kind of hang back, but Rizin looks the biograph right in the eye. He says, "Okay, Dr. King, lay it on me. Tell me why I shouldn't raise a cyborg army and crush Chancellor Graham — or at least give him something to think about."

Tools and Stick are backing up Rizin with their nods. Epps listens carefully, never saying a word.

Dr. King responds in a steady, powerful tone. "Oppressed people can't remain oppressed forever. The yearning for freedom eventually manifests itself, and that is what has happened here."

"We don't want to be second-class citizens," Tools says.

Stick says, "We need to fight."

Dr. King moves closer to Stick. "There's a problem with that way of thinking. You have two opposing forces in the cyborg world. One is a force of complacency, made up in part of cyborgs who, as a result of long years of oppression, are so drained of self-respect and a sense of *somebodyness* that they have accepted being Seconds. The other faction consists of a few highly successful cyborgs, mostly from the Moon, who enjoy a degree of academic and economic security and freedom. But you cyborgs are not working as one. You're insensitive to the pains and joys of one another. You must first hold your team together. And you must be patient with one another."

"How do you know this?" Tools asks Dr. King.

"It's human nature — you are human. I had the same problem in my day — struggles with unity, issues of oppression and complacency. It seems very little has changed since then."

Leanna activates another famous figure, the Dalai Lama, the spiritual leader of Tibet, who enters our space and speaks right up.

"I, too, have been following this conversation." He's calm yet he makes a strong impression and quickly captures our attention. "Once you unite and define your task, you have a simple choice — achieve your goals with violence or nonviolence." Then he turns away from Leanna to face Rizin directly. "If you seek the destruction of the enemy, violence will achieve the goal. If you seek harmony and desire to live next to one another, then you must create, make an effort to make it happen. This is nonviolence."

Epps looks at Rizin, then at Dr. King. "Are you asking us to be martyrs — to let our enemies beat us and kill us?"

"To die for the cause?" I ask.

Dr. King smiles broadly. "The very purpose of nonviolence is to bring peaceful effects. If you bring contrary effects, then you need to change the tactics."

Tools isn't completely convinced. Neither is Stick. Epps looks more and more interested, but she's not ready to commit. There's a grumble in the room. But everyone is still paying close attention.

"You can't negotiate with someone who doesn't want to listen," Stick says.

Epps adds, "We can win a *battle* or a *war*. I want to figure out how to win a *war*. But it's gonna be hard winning a war *nonviolently*."

Rizin never takes his eyes off Epps. But he says to Dr. King, "Sir, I think you may have something here."

Leanna's body relaxes, and for the first time in a while, she looks calmer.

The other cyborgs who've been listening join the conversation.

"War never works," somebody says.

"Neither does sitting around acting peacefully, while others beat you up!" protests another.

"Where do you stand?" Rizin asks Epps.

It takes a moment for her to form her answer. We all wait breathlessly, because we all know how much Epps affects Rizin's decisions. "As impossible as it may be," she says, "I think we have the courage it will take to defeat the Federation *nonviolently*. Even if we die."

Rizin smiles at Epps. "No, we don't have to die. We have to prove we can live together."

To our joy, Rizin is willing to try nonviolence in the upcoming protest. "We'll see how it works," he says.

Leanna and I thumb-thump because we are thrilled.

Over the next week or so, Cyborg City becomes the base of operations for a kickoff protest. Epps has been selected to take over the leadership of the nonviolent approach. She's running into a lot of resistance.

"There are plans under way to hold a Freedom Feast protest, modeled after the lunch counter sit-ins from way back in the 1960s," Epps explains to a large gathering of cyborgs on Cyborg City.

Leanna jumps in. "The demonstrations back then were so awesome. I had to write an essay about them for my history final exam last year. As part of the test, we visited the Greensboro, North Carolina, sit-in, in virtual, then had to write about it. Sandra and I both aced the test."

"Well, ace, tell us what was so awesome about Greensboro," Tools says.

"There were these four African American college kids who walked into a segregated Woolworth's and sat at the lunch counter, waiting to be served. Because they were black, nobody would give them any food. Woolworth's was a 'Whites Only' place — no black customers allowed. After a while, people got mad at the black kids and started yelling at them, pouring hot coffee on their heads and ketchup on their clean clothes, all in an effort to make them leave."

Tools and Stick are listening closely. So are the other cyborgs in the room.

"The college kids who weren't being served kicked their butts, I hope," Stick says.

"Nope — those black students were all about peace. They sat there for hours, quietly, not striking back at all," Leanna explains.

"Were those college students sick in the head? Who takes abuse like that?" Tools asks.

"People who were committed to Dr. King's belief in nonviolent change," Leanna says.

"Later for that!" shouts a cyborg guy whose biofe hands are the size of bricks. He leaves; so do a lot of others. I try to stop them, but there's no use.

Epps tells Leanna not to worry. "Things will come together," she says.

Epps and Rizin have thrown themselves into the movement. For the past week, we've been practicing how to respond to violence in a nonviolent way. We get volunteers enlisting every day. Rizin has been spending his time gathering support for nonviolence, traveling the city, soliciting feedback. Hoping to make a change. Even as a cyborg who needs little sleep, he looks weary lately. Mind-weary.

One day, when we're all hanging out, Rizin does something he hardly ever does — sits down in a chair.

"Anybody ready for a swifting match?" he asks us.

It's been an uncertain few weeks. Some fun will be good. "I'm in," I say.

"Me, too." Leanna's up and eager.

Tools and Stick are also.

We head for the swifting chamber and break up into teams.

Carlos is visiting for the day, so he's my partner, and so is Leanna. We call ourselves The Runaways.

Epps, Tools, and Stick are teammates. They've named their team The Moon Rats. Now I'm into this! Bring it on!

"What rules of play are we using?" asks Leanna.

Tools and Stick snicker. "Anything goes," answers Epps.

Leanna looks at me. "*Anything* goes?"

I nod. "We don't have to do this. . . ."

"Come on," Carlos interrupts. "When we're all weightless, we'll be equal in strength and agility. We can take 'em," he adds, jogging in place.

"You're on," says Leanna, entering the swifting chamber.

Tools lets out a roar intended to scare the boots off all of us as he slams the chamber door and locks us in. Nobody says a word. Slowly, we all begin to rise to our positions along the outer wall, adjust our helmets, suck in oxygen, and prepare to meet our opponents.

Tools is matched against Carlos.

Tools takes the bubble first and dives toward the scoring wall. With a fancy flip he tosses the bubble ball at the 10-point hole, but Carlos, in a smooth sideways move, blocks Tools's toss and the liquid ball misses the goal completely. Carlos's agility catches Tools so off guard, the cyborg is speechless.

This time, Carlos takes the bubble ball. He slowly rises to the top of the chamber, then he spirals downward like an arrow, bounces off the floor, and flips, kicking off Tools's back and at the same time tossing the bubble into the 10-point hole. Score!

"Not fair," shouts Tools. "You pushed off of me. You're not supposed to do that."

"I thought this was an anything-goes game," I say.

"Carlos scored. Period," Rizin rules.

Tools and Stick are glaring.

To take sides with a First against another cyborg is like an unpardonable sin — even if it *is* Carlos.

I'm up next against Stick. He's twice my size and tough as rawhide. His mouth is gloved, so he can't jazz with me. He receives the bubble ball in his hands. I move in to block him, but he kicks out his leg and sends me sailing out of control. My head crashes into the outer wall. I see stars, but I can't stop. I push off and spiral above Stick. Then, coming down in front of him, I flip up and score while hanging upside down.

Stick is mad!

But not as mad as when Leanna runs circles around Epps and scores. Epps soon learns that Leanna is not a good swifter. She's one of the *best*.

Then the teams are tied. Now we have to choose who will play the tie-breaking match. It's decided that Tools will represent The Moon Rats and I will represent The Runaways.

Tools wins the toss for who will make what move first. He chooses to receive.

He scoops up the bubble as it comes out of the tube. Holds it firmly in his gloves. He blocks by shouldering, kicking, and using every illegal maneuver he can against me.

Right then, I remember Leanna's move that she used to beat me the first time we swifted together.

I spin behind Tools. He turns to grab me, but I soar upward. I float down and land on his head. Suddenly, I push off, sending Tools downward and out of control. I move to the goal and score!

"We win!" I shout.

Carlos is so happy. We beat the roughest, toughest cyborgs in the world. We actually beat 'em!

Stick is fuming. Tools is scratching his head. Part of winning is the bragging rights you earn. "Want some of this?" I shout. "Winning sure tastes good! The Runaways rock!"

Rizin calls us together. "What did this game show you, relative to what we've been doing all this time?"

We all stand there, motionless. *Oh, no*, I'm thinking, *Rizin's out to teach one of his lessons. He can be so long-winded, and preachy, and boring!*

But to my surprise he takes a different approach. "Did you notice," he asks, "a cyborg, a clone, and a First won by working together?" Then he leaves us to think about what he'd really said.

THE FREEDOM FEAST

The Freedom Feast protest is today — the first of its kind in modern times. Groups of cyborgs are going to walk into restaurants all over the world and ask for service. They will either be served or not. If not, they will sit quietly until they're forced to leave. We've practiced every possible situation we might encounter. We are ready. I am so ready!

Thousands of cyborgs have come to join us in the Cyborg City demonstrations. They are filling restaurants all over the city. Rizin and Leanna stay at headquarters to monitor what's happening all over the world.

Epps is so nervous not knowing what is going to happen.

Leanna shouts to everyone as they head away to their farcars. "Don't forget your training. Think nonviolence."

"We are heading to Café Tacuba in the old district," Epps announces.

Tools, Stick, and I are assigned to a group of sixteen other cyborgs. Most of them look like regular Firsts. Tools and Stick are obvious Moonborgs — the ones Firsts are terrified of.

The restaurant is lovely, very upscale, decorated with colored tiles. Stained glass windows and old-fashioned furniture please the eyes. Tamale and enchilada aromas dance out of the kitchen. "Stick, you hungry?" I ask.

"Sure am," he answers, moving to sit down at an open table.

"Don't you have any manners?" the hostess says to Stick. "Our sign says wait to be seated!" Then she looks at his mouth in his hand. She gags and hurries away.

The other staff members vanish and guests drop their heads as if too scared to look at us. The owner of the restaurant appears. In controlled rage, he says, "What do you want?"

"What do most people want in a restaurant? A good meal," says Epps, taking a seat. We all join her. Suddenly, people begin to ease out. Most without finishing their meals.

"I don't want any problems," says the owner. I can hear the fear and hatred he feels for cyborgs.

We all sit silently, looking straight ahead. The few remaining patrons sit in stunned silence.

"Epps, it's working," I say.

Finally, one of the waiters sets some salsa and chips on the table. Stick puts his mouth over the bowl of chips, and, like a vacuum cleaner, sucks all of them out of the bowl. Without hesitation, he sucks up the bowl of salsa, too.

"Well, was it any good?" Tools asks.

Stick raises his hand to Tools. "Yep, the best I've had in a while." Then, using his other hand, he wipes his mouth.

"Disgusting," one of the other patrons says in complete horror. She throws down her napkin and leaves.

I don't know why the owner decides to do it, but he sighs deeply, then waves the rest of the staff to wait on us. Without further incident we all order a snack and eat. We pay the bill and leave as orderly as possible.

Outside, we are so excited. We are proud and happy. Nonviolence has worked.

I contact Rizin back at command. "It's going really well. No fights yet," Rizin reports.

"It went well with us," I say. "We're heading to the cyborg and student demonstration at the St. Louis Gateway to the West Arch. See you and Leanna there."

As soon as we reach the West Arch grounds, I see that Federation Special Forces have set up a barrier. One of the guards pushes Tools, who instinctively pushes back. Immediately, another officer takes hold of him.

Remembering my training in nonviolent resistance, I step forward, speaking in a slow, deliberate manner. "Sir, we mean no harm to anyone. We just want to be heard."

The officer stops instantly and stands so still, I wonder if he is a biograph. He lets go of Tools, who quickly scampers away. All I see are the officer's eyes glaring at me from behind his raised helmet visor.

Finally, he speaks. "Huey, is that you?"

Only my family calls me Huey. Especially my brother.

No. It can't be.

The soldier grabs me by my arm and pulls me into a nearby alley. He rips off his helmet. "Huey, it's me, Tobias, your big brother — Toby." He reaches out and pulls me into an embrace. "I'm so glad to see you."

I let him hug me. Tightly. It feels so good to touch my brother. He isn't a dream.

I'm really here with my big brother, Tobias Ye. "It's been years since we last saw each other," I say.

We are both quiet again. What do you say to a memory?

In the background I can hear that Rizin has come to the protest site. The cyborg demonstrators are protesting the Wholer Act. "We are not going to accept second-class citizenship any longer," says Rizin. "The laws are discriminatory. Change the cyborg laws."

"Change the cyborg laws!" the crowd chants.

Toby turns to me. "That's your guardian, right?"

"You bet, and he's been a good one since . . . since . . . Dad died." Toby can't take his eyes off me. "How do you know about Rizin?"

Toby explains. "Chancellor Graham became my guardian

when Dad and Mom died. He and Rizin were good friends at one time, then Rizin became a cyborg and dropped him as a friend. He's always been hurt about it."

That's not the way it happened, but Toby thinks that it's true. So I can't be angry with him. But I have a thousand questions for him.

"When did Mom die?" I ask.

"Five years ago," Toby says, shaking his head as if to dismiss a bad thought. "It was hard for her. The only thing she wanted was to see you. And when you refused to come for a visit, it broke her heart."

"What?" I'm shocked. "I was *never* asked to visit Mom. And why would she want to see me? *She* abandoned *me* when I needed her most."

"Huey, you aren't making sense. Mom loved you dearly. After Dad died, Mr. Graham counseled Mom that it would be better for you to go to the Cyborg Center for Labor and Industry."

I tell Toby, "I was there until I graduated. But I spent vacations with Rizin on the Moon. The Moonborgs became my friends and family."

"You abandoned Mom and me for *them*?" There's a smirk on Toby's face that chills me.

"Mom sends me off to a school, hundreds of miles away, and never comes to see me, and never attempts to contact me in any way, and you say *I* abandoned *you*! How dare you try to blame me."

"You never got Mom's virtual messages? She sent one every week." Toby believes every word he's saying.

"I never heard from her. Nothing."

"You mean you've gone years without hearing from us? You thought we had abandoned you? That must have been awful. I know it was for Mom. But the chancellor said you didn't want to see us. You had written us off and didn't want to communicate with us."

"The chancellor told you that? Well, he lied. He never spoke to me about a thing. That man is not to be trusted. He's a snake."

Toby pulls himself tall. "Hold on. The chancellor has been a good friend to me. He's shepherded me through some of the best schools in the world and now I'm in the Federation Special Forces. I won't have you calling him names, even if you are my brother."

"Good to know where you stand," I say, feeling disappointed.

Epps suddenly comes into the alley. She looks frightened. Her eyes dart from Toby to me. She's tentative. "Houston, we've been looking for you. Are you okay?"

I nod.

She speaks slowly, "We're getting ready to go." She hands me a sign that reads RIGHTS AND FREEDOM FOR ALL!

"Coming," I answer. Then turning to Toby I try to smile. "Good seeing you, Big Bro. Maybe in another ten years our paths will cross again."

"I hope not that long. I think we need to talk more. Get to the truth of what's been going on. Look, here are some untraceable commglasses," says Toby. "I can be contacted on them. Call if you need me for anything."

"Okay." I don't expect to ever use the glasses, but I keep them anyway.

CAPTURED

Leanna has gone ahead. Epps and I press through the crowd, looking for her. I look toward the podium. Up at the stage and to my left, I see Chief Justice Granbury! *What is he doing here?* And to my horror, I see Leanna sitting next to him.

My whole body goes limp. I know what she's getting ready to do. I haven't told her that I suspect Granbury is not on our side. I'm trying not to panic. I feel Apache quivering. "No, Apache," I say to my Familiar. "I don't need you now. Quiet."

I begin pressing harder to get through the crowd. People resist me.

Leanna steps to the podium before I can get to her. "My name is Leanna Deberry. I am the daughter of Annette Deberry. And I am the clone of a twin sister who died early in life."

Suddenly, the crowd gets quiet. People stop, except me. I am steadily moving toward the stage. Leanna's getting ready to make a huge mistake, thinking this is what she's supposed to be doing as a Custodian of The Liberty Bell Movement. I don't think The O intended her to martyr herself for the cause.

"No, I don't have purple or orange skin," she continues.

"I'm not bald, and I'm not a mindless creature who has a life expectancy of thirteen years. I will be fourteen, come this summer. Also, I am an honor student in my school and a leader among my friends. I am evidence that my mother and my pediatrician are not guilty of treason. They just want clones to have rights and freedom as sentient beings."

There are murmurs. "You don't look like a clone to me," shouts a demonstrator.

"How can you prove you're a clone?" asks another.

I can hear the challenge in their words.

Leanna holds up her hands. The crowd settles down. I continue to move toward the front of the crowd. Leanna keeps talking. "There are those who have questioned my authenticity. They say I have to be examined by Federation authorities before I can be admitted as evidence that infant cloning is possible."

At this point, Granbury steps forward. He stands beside her.

"No, Leanna! No!" I shout. She doesn't hear me over the crowd. I keep moving ahead, trying hard not to panic. Apache is twitching to spring. It takes all the control I can muster to keep him in check. I'm still too far away.

"I am voluntarily turning myself over to Chief Justice Granbury, who has agreed to do the necessary testing to prove my case," Leanna's saying.

Granbury speaks up. "Please let it be known that Leanna Deberry has been taken into custody at her own request. It is her hope and ours to prove once and for all if she is a clone or a hoax."

This has all been planned so well. It takes seconds for Leanna to be shoved into a waiting farcar and whisked away. Gone. Captured!

Epps catches up with me. "What is going on, for Pete's sake?"

"I've got to find Rizin. Leanna is in terrible danger."

Together we strategize.

"Maybe Granbury will take care of her," Tools says, hopefully.

"You know better," Epps says, spitting out her words. "You've got a biofe ear. Didn't you hear Granbury's lie?"

There is silence.

Just then the commglasses Toby's given me signal. My brother's trying to reach me. I dig the secure glasses out of my backpack and put them on. Toby comes into view.

"Look, I'm risking my career by doing this, but I know Leanna Deberry is part of your group," my brother begins. "Granbury had no choice but to betray your cause. The authorities discovered he was a member of The Liberty Bell Movement and they gave him two alternatives. Either help them or lose everything and go to prison."

"What about Leanna?" I ask.

"They've sent her to the Topas Corporation's Marketing Center, down in Ushuaia, Argentina. I'm sending your glasses the coordinates and entry codes for Topas."

"How'd you get the codes?" I ask.

"You don't want to know. Just go. But remember, once you get in, you're on your own. I've done all I can."

"Thanks, Toby," I say, feeling proud that my brother is helping our cause.

Toby's gone as easily as he's come. I'm on overload. Too many emotions bombarding me. Too much to think about.

"Where did you get those commglasses?" Epps asks.

I tell Epps all about Toby. She is listening, shaking her head, trying to make sense of everything.

"Toby says Leanna is at Topas, in Argentina," I tell her.

"Are you sure you can *trust* your brother?" Epps asks.

"Tobias is all we have." I pound my fist on the table. "Let's stop talking. Every minute we waste could mean life or death for Leanna. Let's go, and let's go united."

RUBy and Carlos pick us up at dawn at Cyborg City. By using the coordinates we were given by my brother, RUBy goes to Ushuaia, the last city at the tip of Argentina. She goes into chameleon mode some distance from the Topas Center. Before I leave the ship, Rizin tosses a mechanical-looking spider into my hand. Rizin, Tools, and the rest of the team are wearing face masks.

Epps steps up to me and takes the black-silver spider from my hand. She places it over my biofe eye. The spider digs its legs and body into my face. What was once the body of the spider is now my eye. It glows bright red. I'm confused at first. Then I understand. I can see what Rizin can see. I can see what Tools sees. Epps steps back, smiling. "You are a Moonborg now with a real battle biofe eye."

I can see everything that everyone else is seeing without being confused. It's like we are all truly one.

"Courage defeats the impossible," Rizin says to us all. We respond to him by repeating our battle cry.

Without saying another word, we slip off the ship.

I'm dizzy with fear. Are we going to be too late? Have they done anything to Leanna? If so, what?

Following Rizin's lead, we approach the building but stay out of view of surveillance. With the codes to open the door, we enter without difficulty.

"That was easy," I whisper.

"Topas doesn't care about anybody getting in. It's the getting out that's the challenge," Rizin says. "They change exit codes every hour."

Rizin leaves Stick and Tools at the exit. "Hold the door open or we'll be trapped inside," he whispers. His crew nods.

The lighting is dim. Our battle eyes allow us to see clearly down the corridor, through the walls and doors. I hear my eye talking to me, identifying objects as I gaze on them. The many rooms and connecting corridors are filled with giant glass tubes, some larger than a swimming pool. Inside them are thousands of clones in various stages of adult maturity, a floating nursery of bodies. My stomach wants to give back breakfast, but I fight to keep myself from vomiting. I'm not the only one this place is getting to.

"This is awful," says Epps.

Rizin grunts and looks away.

We hear voices down the hallway. We scale along the wall until we see several hundred purple clones seated in a large room. Their eyes stare straight ahead, lifeless. Several Topas workers are methodically placing chips behind the clones' ears.

"Those are the behavior chips they put in clones to keep them compliant," Epps says.

Corridors are filled with suspended orange and purple body parts. It gets creepier and creepier.

"Over here," says Rizin. He's found Leanna in a small room at the end of a short hallway. Epps stays back while Rizin and I go get Leanna.

She's in a dark room by herself. "Leanna," I whisper. "We're here for you. Can you walk?"

"Houston?" She sounds groggy and confused. I'm worried about what these maniacs have done to her.

"Come on, Leanna," says Rizin. "I'll carry you." He lifts her in his biofe arms and heads out of the room. As soon as he crosses the threshold, an alarm sounds.

"Run for it!" shouts Rizin.

Suddenly, guards are dashing down the hallway, chasing us and closing in. "We should have dropped bread crumbs," says Epps. "Which way did we come in?"

"This way," I say, heading down a passage that looks like one we had taken. I really wasn't sure. Thank goodness Rizin chose to run the opposite way.

We follow him and almost make it to the exit door, when security guards block us. Others are closing in from behind. "Tools," Rizin calls. "Catch."

With his powerful biofe arms Rizin tosses Leanna over the guards' heads, and Tools catches her as easily as he might catch a baseball.

In the next second, Rizin turns to meet the advancing guards.

Epps leaps in with a scream, and so do I. We use our

mental and physical cyborg strength to speedily take out the front line. But other guards rush us. We need help.

Rizin touches his shoulder. A fully hooded king cobra appears, hissing and threatening the guards. By using his Familiar as a shield, Rizin takes out three or four guards and moves a little closer to the door, where Stick and Tools are holding it open.

"Hurry, Rizin! The door is trying to close. We aren't going to be able to hold it open much longer," Tools shouts.

"We're coming as fast as we can," I say. I touch my shoulder and my Familiar leaps to life. "Apache, over here," I call. The big wolf crouches and waits for a good time to strike. When he attacks, my opponents scatter.

Epps releases her Familiar, a green-eyed jaguar. One roar sends the guards scuffling to get out of range, but not before the jaguar mauls a guard. It gives Epps time to rush to the door. She moves so fast, she seems invisible.

I see Rizin ahead of me. A guard is slipping up behind him. "In back of you!" I yell, forgetting Rizin sees what I see.

He turns without hesitating, kicking and jabbing his attacker. He's almost at the door, when suddenly biobots attack from front and back.

Where are they coming from? My heart is beating fast and it's hard to breathe. But I'm not afraid. Apache is pumping me up, and I'm finding the courage I need to keep fighting.

A biobot snaps its razor-sharp teeth into my biofe leg. I feel nothing.

I've got just enough time to flip over several of the metal monsters to get in better position to rush for the door. I'd be a goner already if the Familiars weren't holding them off. I am so proud of my wolf.

Epps and Rizin are helping Tools and Stick keep the door open. They are coaxing me. "Hurry, Houston. Hurry."

I hear Rizin order Stick to carry Leanna to RUBy and be ready to go on command. That makes me happy. Leanna is back in safe hands again. I feel myself weakening. My turbo-gun is nearly drained.

As strong as the three cyborgs are, the door is putting tremendous pressure on them. I see the door sliding. "We can't hold on any longer," says Rizin through clenched teeth.

Suddenly, I think about Captain Shackleton. He was in a no-win situation. But he made a decision that seemed ridiculous at the time. He knew his men and knew that they were capable.

So now in this impossible situation, I've got to make a decision. And I don't have forever to think about it. The biobots are closing in.

"Go!" I shout. "I'll make it somehow."

"No," calls Rizin. "We're coming to get you now!"

"Stop. Think. If you come for me, who will hold the door open? Go, please. Just promise you won't forget where you left me." I'm scared to death, and I know this is probably the end for me, but I'm hoping that we'll have the luck of Shackleton and get out of this thing without losing anybody.

Rizin doesn't answer.

"Good-bye, Houston. You bet I won't forget!" answers Tools.

After bringing home my wolf, I'm exhausted. I drop to my knees and hold up my arms in surrender. The biobots fall upon me like vultures. That's the last thing I remember.

THE TRUTH

I wake up in a hospital room, fighting to sit up. I settle down some when I see my brother sitting by my bed, nodding. He looks so much like Dad — same squared-off chin, same tilt of his head.

"Hey," I manage to whisper. My head feels like somebody's been inside it mining for moon rocks.

Toby says, "Thank goodness you're all right."

"Thank goodness I'm *alive*! I thought I was gonna wake up dead."

Toby ruffles my hair and memories of sharing a room with my big brother flood my brain. Whenever I got into trouble, Toby was always there to pull me out of it. Seems right that he should be here now. My head throbs, and I groan again.

"What have they done to me?" I feel sick to my stomach.

"Those biobots whipped your butt," Toby says, shaking his head. "Chancellor Graham commanded that you be brought here and he ordered a brain drain to retrieve information from you."

"Well, I guess I'm fried. What I know, Graham now knows. Everything."

While I'm thinking about how Graham is going to use the information he's gotten from me, the door swings open. Joe Spiller comes in to get me.

"Awake, huh?" he snarls.

Instinctively, I touch Apache.

"Don't try anything stupid," Spiller says. "Don't make me have to do something bad to you or your pet Familiar."

"Still Mr. Charm, I see."

Spiller gets me released from the hospital and takes me to the chancellor's office. Toby is there when I arrive.

Spiller says, "You won't be so smart for long. You're in our house now."

Taylor Graham stays seated at his desk. Toby is standing at attention by the window.

The T is on behind him. Crowds of Firsts and Seconds are peacefully protesting the treatment of clones in cities all over the world. "End injustice," the protesters are chanting.

Graham says, "Well, young man, you seem to be pleased with the mess your people have created."

"You should know," I say. "You've drained what's in my mind."

Graham smirks. "The data we drained from your itsy-bitsy brain yielded some good information, especially about that criminal Li Rizin and your ungrateful brother over there. More is being interpreted as we speak."

"Then you have to know how much I despise who you are, what you represent, and what you did to my family," I say.

Graham's face is filled with disgust. "Let me explain something about you and your family. When you became a cyborg, you became a drag on your family. With you at home, your brother would never have gotten into the fine schools he's attended. I was never able to convince your father, but when he was gone, I was able to show your mother that she was doing what was best for both sons. I told her you'd be better off at the cyborg school, and I promised to help Toby get a military education."

"Permission to speak," says Toby.

Graham nods.

Toby is hesitant, but he starts peppering him with questions. "Why didn't you allow Mom's communications to reach Huey? He was so young and without a family. He thought we had deserted him! And why did you tell us he didn't want to hear from us and refused to communicate?" Toby measures his words. Softly, he asks, "What kind of sick person would do something so heinous?"

"I did it because I loved your father. I owed it to him to take care of his family, and this was the best way to do it."

"Dad died in a farcar accident," I say. "He chose to die rather than be made a cyborg. That let me know he didn't want to be like me."

Graham laughs. "The four of us — Spiller, Rizin, your father, and I — were the best of friends in the Special Forces. We were young and wild, and full of hopes and dreams. But we were good soldiers, among the best, with great possibilities for our future. Then Rizin was made a cyborg. Your father was willing to sacrifice his career to help him. But I saw what happened to both of them. When your father was hurt in the farcar accident and was lying there unconscious, the medics said they could save him by using biofe parts. I told them he didn't want that even if it meant his death."

I can hardly get the question out of my mouth, but I manage. "Dad didn't make that decision for himself?"

"You killed our father," Toby says.

I don't need my biofe ear to hear the fury in my brother's words.

"Your father would have been as good as dead living as a cyborg," Graham says.

"So then you got Mom to get rid of me and you mentored Toby," I say. "Now I know why Rizin hates you so much. Does he know you killed his best friend?"

"All Rizin knows is that I used my persuasion to help him get that good position on the Moon. As long as he stays on the Moon, I have no problem with him. But now that he's chosen to get into the protest movement, I will have no choice but to get rid of him."

Toby's fists are clenched at his sides. "I believed in you," he says. "I trusted you! But it's all been a lie! Consider me your enemy!"

"I'll tell you what's even sicker, Graham," I say. "You believe you're right."

Suddenly, Rizin's holograph appears in the room. RUBy has hacked into the system. "Graham," says Rizin. "I'm coming in to get Houston. We can save a lot of trouble for us both if you just let him go. You've got what you want."

Graham leans back in his chair confidently. "You can have Houston and his loser brother. You're right — I have just what I need. Through our brain drain we now have information that will change everything — the confessions of a cyborg."

A MEMO TO THE MASSES

From: The World Federation of Nations

Re: Runaways

ATTENTION: This memorandum is to alert everyone on Earth and on surrounding planets about the recent escape of five cyborgs, a clone, and a First, via spaceship.

The fugitives in question are cyborgs Li Rizin and his teenage charge, Houston Ye, and Leanna Deberry, a clone who is the daughter of Liberty Bell Movement member Dr. Annette Deberry, currently under house arrest and awaiting trial by a World Supreme Court grand jury. Leanna Deberry, Li Rizin, and Houston Ye are accompanied by three cyborgs, a Dr. Epps, and two others who go by the names of Stick and Tools. Carlos Pace, a First and son of Dr. Marcus Pace, is also with the group.

Each of these fugitives now has a bounty of $1,000,000 on his or her head if captured alive; $500,000 if turned in dead.

The World Federation of Nations has appointed officer Joseph Spiller, from the newly formed Bureau of Security and Discipline (BSD), to lead the search for the capture of these runaways. Please direct any information to Spiller at BSD headquarters.

TIMELINE OF THE FUTURE

2083–2171

2083

The World Federation of Nations (WFN) is formed after the end of a major world war that killed millions and nearly devastated the planet. The WFN's purpose is to manage all resources responsibly and to share, protect, and defend all profits earned from Moon and Mars mining with the nations of the world.

2084

The WFN establishes the definition of a cyborg: *All persons who have been enhanced with three or more biofe, or synthetic body or organ replacements, shall be classified as three-fifths of a human being, or a cyborg.*

Moon mining begins.

Construction of Mars base begins.

2096

Mars mining begins.

2102

Infant cloning is abolished worldwide. Cloning has proven to be unstable. Baby clones' second-generation cells deteriorate very fast, so by age thirteen they usually die of a heart attack.

Dr. David Montgomery, Leanna's great-grandfather, develops an adult cloning machine. The Topas Corporation buys the patent and begins producing adult clones.

It is suspected that Dr. Montgomery had a stabilizer for cloning, which would enable infants to be safely cloned and allow clone children to possess more of the traits of human children. It is believed that if not programmed, clone children would be no different from any other child.

Adult cloning has become a way of life, even though the life expectancy of a clone is still thirteen years. Cloning has evolved.

People are beginning to question the abilities and psychic condition of clones, asking questions such as *Are clones sentient? Are they self-aware?*

2130

John P. Haversham, Director of the Bureau of Cyborg Affairs, issues the Cyborg Act on October 7. Cyborgs are reduced to second-class citizens, without the rights or privileges of humans.

2154

Houston Ye is born.

2158

Leanna Deberry is born.

2159

Li Rizin enters the World Federation of Nations Special Forces with his friends Joe Spiller, Taylor Graham, and John Ye.

2161

Houston Ye is in a boating accident. Houston becomes a cyborg.

Li Rizin becomes a battlefield cyborg.

2162

Li Rizin is involved in a minor cyborg uprising to protest housing discrimination. His former friend Taylor Graham intercedes on Rizin's behalf, and instead of being sent to jail, Rizin is transferred to the Moon mining colony.

2163

Houston's father is fatally wounded in a farcar accident. He chooses death rather than become a cyborg. Houston is sent to the Cyborg Center for Labor and Industry, a boarding school for cyborgs. Houston is separated from his family.

2170

Taylor Graham is elected Chancellor of The WFN.

The Liberty Bell Movement leaders are arrested and charged with treason. Leanna's mother, Dr. Annette Deberry, and her pediatrician, Dr. Anatol Ayala, are arrested.

By 2170 clones are color coded to designate their work status, or "station." For example, orange clones are general laborers; purple clones are academics who work with children and in the field of education.

Leanna learns she is a clone and the product of a baby-cloning experiment. As such, she has fallen under the scrutiny of The WFN and is forced to flee her home.

Leanna meets Houston on a Gypsy City floating junkyard, a safe place on her escape route. Their friendship is rocky at first.

Leanna hides on Atlantis, a biosphere. She learns from experience what it means to be a clone.

Houston and Leanna meet Carlos and RUBy, a spaceship prototype powered by an extremely advanced Artificial Intelligence (AI).

It is established that the World Supreme Court will be petitioned to hear Leanna's case, which will prove or disprove the legitimacy of clones as sentient beings.

Li Rizin gets involved with Leanna and The Liberty Bell Movement.

Joe Spiller and his biobots find Leanna at Atlantis. With the help of Houston, she escapes. Carlos offers to help Leanna and Houston if he can travel with them. Carlos, Leanna, and Houston flee to the Moon with RUBy, the Federation's deep-space model ship.

2171

The Wholer organization is established on the Internet. Membership triples after a series of demonstrations against the Clone Codes and the Cyborg Act, which the clone and cyborg communities call unjust.

At this point in history, many supremacist groups, such as the Wholers, model some of their tactics on the Back-to-Africa movement of the nineteenth century. The Back-to-Africa movement, also known as the Colonization movement, originated in the United States and encouraged those of African descent to return to the African homelands of their ancestors.

YESTERDAY....
TOMORROW

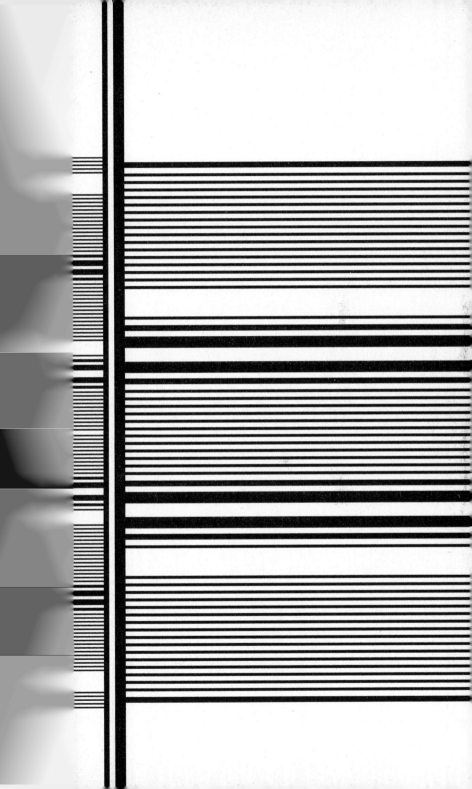

YESTERDAY

In 1871, after the Civil War and slavery had ended, the western frontier became an ideal place where former slaves, former Confederate and Union soldiers, Native Americans, and Mexicans could live together peacefully. The frontiersmen were not judged because of their beliefs, their ethnicity, or their lifestyle. Because of its rural nature, extreme weather conditions, and wildlife, the West could be harsh and unforgiving. People had to depend on one another and their horses. The horse was a loyal friend and constant companion to frontiersmen.

TOMORROW

In 2170, when cyborgs and clones begin to fight for equal rights, the Moon is the new frontier. Cyborgs and clones coexist peacefully with Firsts. Discrimination and class system oppression are not yet part of the culture.

YESTERDAY

Long ago, in the 1600s, when people feared witches and witchcraft, animals — especially cats and birds — were called Familiars. They were considered evil creatures under the control of a witch. Unable to resist the witch's power, the Familiar did the witch's bidding by spying on humans and protecting and defending the witch.

TOMORROW

A cyborg's Familiar in 2170 is a devoted companion, similar to a frontiersman's horse. And the Familiars of tomorrow protect and defend like the Familiars of legend. The mixing of animal and human DNA allows the cyborg to experience the power of the creature chosen to be his or her Familiar.

YESTERDAY

The Civil Rights Movement began when Americans decided that justice and freedom should be granted to all citizens equally. Ms. Rosa Parks of Montgomery, Alabama, refused to obey the unfair law that black passengers had to ride in the backs of buses. She was arrested but released on bail. In December 1955 the Montgomery Bus Boycott followed, led by Dr. Martin Luther King, Jr., who believed in passive resistance. The success of the bus boycott led to other peaceful protests: marches, sit-ins, boycotts, and demonstrations.

TOMORROW

In 2171, the Cyborg Civil Rights Movement is sparked by the Wholer Act. Others join the movement, which is based on Dr. King's philosophy of nonviolent protests. Even though the WFN forces are unnecessarily brutal, the cyborgs' movement remains passive — but very aggressive in their persistence.

YESTERDAY

Wolves have been misrepresented in literature, plays, and films. The Big Bad Wolf was an exaggeration that caused the wolf to be hunted and killed to the point of extinction. Wolves are animals that live in families, or packs. Contrary to popular belief, wolves are not vicious killers. They hunt to eat. An alpha male and alpha female govern the pack with strict rules of conduct and absolute authority. The survival of the pack depends upon loyalty, obedience, and order. Those wolves that live outside the family are called lone wolves, but usually these loners are looking for a pack of their own.

TOMORROW

Liz Rizin chooses the wolf to be Houston's Familiar in 2170. He believes the wolf's character matches Houston's desire to be a leader. And like the lone wolf, Houston is searching for a

YESTERDAY

For centuries, supremacy groups grew out of the mistaken idea that one's race, religion, creed, nationality, gender, financial status, or educational credentials made one superior to all others. Among the most feared and dangerous supremacists were hate groups such as the Nazi Party in Germany, led by Adolf Hitler, who was in power from 1933 until April 1945, and the Ku Klux Klan, organized in the United States after the Civil War.

TOMORROW

The Wholers of 2171 are members of a supremacy group who define themselves as "whole" humans — no mechanical or plastic parts. Wholers are modeled after hate groups from the nineteenth and twentieth centuries. Their goals are to oppress those they consider "lower" than they are and to promote their own "wholeness."

ARE YOU BRAVE ENOUGH FOR CLONE CODES #3?

There is a wicked system of operation inside the Topas Corporation, where clones are produced. Only authorized Topas officials are allowed inside. Only they, along with the clones themselves, know what happens within the walls of the world's largest and most powerful cloning company. The next book of The Clone Codes begins with Carlos Pace, who gives a glimpse into this alternate — and strange — reality.

THE MAKING

The water is warm, like waves in a water park. Rolling waves toss me as I play.

I feel sleepy. I'm floating in something thick and gooey. The stuff is very sweet as it touches my tongue and fills the insides of my nose. It's sweeter than syrup. Too sweet. I try to spit it out, but the taste won't go away.

It's hard to breathe as my mouth fills with more and more syrupy stuff. The inside of my nose starts to burn. Two tubes have been pushed up in them so that I can breathe in all this gooeyness.

I try to stay calm, but I'm gagging. I keep my mouth shut, not wanting to swallow the warm syrup.

How long have I been here?

I'm so tired. Did I fall asleep again?

Oh, do my eyes hurt. The bright lights stab at me. It's worse than someone poking my eyes with a stick. I can't move my arms and legs in all this thickness.

I can't move my hands, either. They've been tied with ropes.

I'm stuck in some kind of glass jar, with wires connected to my body. I start to cry, and soon sleep takes over.

When I wake, I'm choking, gagging even harder. And I'm shivering. The syrup is gone. But now I'm in salty water. A tube pushes icy liquid into my throat.

My body knows to swallow. My stomach fills quickly.

There are no more wires, just the tubes in my mouth and nose.

When I glance at my hands, I see they are bright orange. My *whole body* is orange.

There are voices in my head now, talking loudly.

This clone is #9767.

This clone wants to work.

This clone is happy.

This clone is #9767.

This clone wants to work.

This clone is happy.

This clone is #9767.

This clone wants to work.

This clone is happy.

"Stop!" I scream.

Newbery Honor winner Patricia C. McKissack has collaborated on many critically acclaimed books with her husband, Fredrick L. McKissack. Together, they are the authors of numerous award winners, including *Rebels Against Slavery: American Slave Revolts* and *Black Hands, White Sails: The Story of African-American Whalers*, both Coretta Scott King Honor Books, and *Sojourner Truth: Ain't I a Woman?* a Coretta Scott King Honor Book and winner of the Boston Globe/Horn Book Award. Patricia and Fredrick McKissack live in St. Louis, Missouri.

John McKissack, the son of Patricia and Fredrick, is a licensed mechanical engineer. *The Clone Codes* marks his debut as a writer. John is married to Michelle McKissack, and they are the parents of three sons, Peter, James Everett, and John. He resides in Memphis, Tennessee.

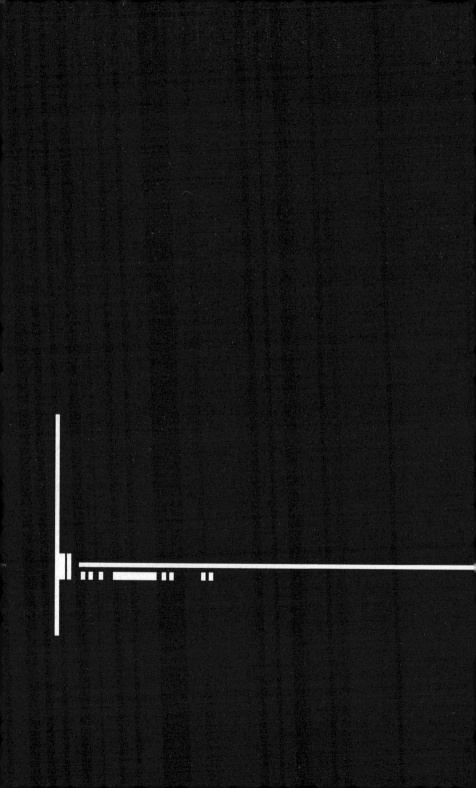

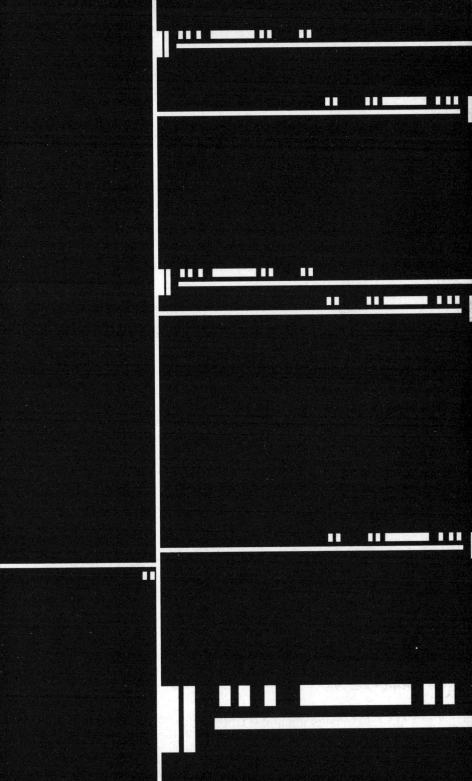

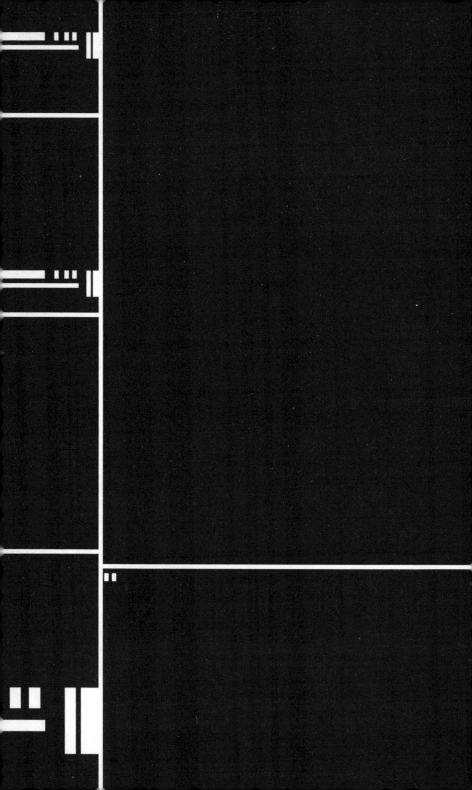